BOOK TWO

KEEP me

USA TODAY BESTSELLING AUTHORS
J.L. BECK & C. HALLMAN

Copyright © 2019 by J.L. Beck C. Hallman

All rights reserved.

No part of this book may be reproduced in any form or by any electronic or mechanical means, including information storage and retrieval systems, without written permission from the author, except for the use of brief quotations in a book review.

Cover Design by: C. Hallman

Editing: Word Nerd

PROLOGUE

ander

THE GUN WAS heavy in my sweaty hands. I wasn't afraid of killing my father. I'm sure he knew it was coming far before I decided to do it, but tonight was the night. He wouldn't hurt Damon and me ever again, and I'd be fucking sure of it.

I walked down the dimly lit hallway, and then down the steps toward the patio.

"I've always thought you were the weakest link of this family. It seems the beatings never really did anything to you. You've still shown weakness...and weakness just isn't acceptable in our family." My father's voice carries through the house as he talks down to Damon.

Anger surges deep inside me, on the verge of exploding outward. I see the glint of a gun in the moonlight that pours from the night sky as I turn the corner.

"You're a piece of shit. A monster who will never amount to anything," Damon spits. "And someday when you're old and gray, I'm going to treat you the same fucking way you treated me and Xander."

I can't see my father's face, but I'm positive there is a cruel smirk on his lips. I wonder if this is the moment I've been dreading. I knew it was coming for a while but I'm not sure this is it until I see my father raise the gun and point it at Damon.

There's not a damn bone within my body that is scared of killing my father. After all, this is what he had planned for me, for us, right? I wait, watching, to see what his next move is.

"You won't be doing shit but letting the worms and bugs crawl through your decaying body." My father flicks the safety and aims the gun. I don't really understand why Damon still stands there, but he does, his eyes never wavering from Dad's.

"Don't make fun about it, just fucking do it," Damon grits out, darkness resonating out of him. As soon as the words are said, everything seems to slow down.

I don't know why Damon and our father are fighting or what it was even about, but when I see him squeeze the trigger on his gun, I know I have to end him. He'd hurt us for so many years, abused and killed those we loved.

He was the real monster, and I was ready to put a bullet in his head.

Lifting my gun, I watched in horror as our father shot Damon in the shoulder. Maybe it was his intention, or maybe it wasn't. I don't really know. I didn't really care or stop to ask. In fact, I was past caring. He deserved to die.

Flicking the safety off, my eyes met Damon's and for a fraction of a second, he sees me. The real me, the man who had spent years taking *beatings so his life could be easier. The poison of this world was slowly seeping into my veins, but it didn't have to taint Damon.*

I pulled the trigger without another thought, watching as the bullet went straight into my father's chest. When he started to fall over, his knees slamming onto the hard ground, I walked over to Damon, gripping him by the arm. I looked straight into my father's eyes, right into the dark orbs that had promised me nothing but death and pain all my life.

"Looks like the worms and bugs are going to be crawling through you soon." Then I shot him again, right in the stomach. If the shot to the chest didn't kill him, then he'd most likely bleed out. His mouth popped open and a vacant look appeared in his eyes.

You could say that was the day I became fully invested in the man I was —the dark monster he had crafted and molded me to be.

The day I took over the Rossi Empire.

1

lla

A MILLION SCENARIOS are running rampant in my mind as I try and sit up and stare into vacant space. Each one has the same ending, with me dead.

Tied up in an empty room, I gaze down at my body. Fear trickles down my spine when I take in the revealing lingerie that covers little pieces of my creamy white skin.

Who dressed me up in these?

I'd never wear anything like this... never.

There's a pounding directly behind my eyes like I got hit by a bus or something. I might have. I don't remember much of how I got here or even where I am.

I was looking for my sister, my sole purpose in life since she'd gone missing a month ago. She is the only family I have left, and I have a compelling need to find her.

For so long, that was all I could think about... finding her, making sure she was okay, but now I've gotten myself into something dangerous, something scary.

My surroundings are eerily quiet, like there is no one else in the bedroom, or maybe even the whole house? I don't know if that makes me feel better or worse, to be left alone in silence.

It's merely a waiting game now... and I wait... with bated breath, for whoever did this to show themselves.

My thoughts are foggy as I tug on the restraints again, praying just this once that I can break free. I cry out in pain when all they do is dig deeper into my already raw skin. My body aches, even as I try and stretch my muscles.

I'm never going to get out of here.

I'm never going to find my sister.

The tears slip from my eyes with ease, sliding down my cheeks. Each drop lands coldly on my skin. For a long time, I just lie there on the cold floor, with no sound other than my breathing and soft sniffles.

That is until another sound breaks the silence. Approaching footsteps from outside the door have me on high alert. My gaze lifts to the wooden door. Waiting. Watching. The footsteps are faint at first but are definitely coming closer... heading straight for me.

They stop right in front of the door. My ears perk up, and my body trembles slightly. I wonder who is going to be on the other side of that door? Part of me wishes it's someone who's here to save me, but I know it isn't.

The door handle turns, and the door opens with a loud creak. The sound startles me even though I knew it was coming.

A large man appears in the doorway. Tall, with broad shoulders. My gaze lifts from the floor and to him, and my blood runs cold. Even though I've never seen this man before, nor met him, I know he is here to hurt me, maybe even kill me.

His eyes are dark, darker than black, and there is no sympathy in them at all, only darkness. An evil grin tugs on his thin lips... This man is the devil in human form, and his sinister smile tells me he is going to enjoy every single thing he does.

A tear runs down my cheek without my permission. I don't want to show him how afraid I am. I don't want to be weak, not for this monster.

"Oh, sweet Ella, don't cry yet, it's far too early for that. We haven't even started." He takes a step toward me, and I recoil, wanting so badly to escape him. His smile widens when he sees me try to scurry backward.

"I will enjoy those tears more as I'm licking them off your face when I'm balls deep inside of you and you are begging me to stop."

I was prepared to beg for my life, even if it made me weak. I was going to do it, but now that I've seen and heard this monster, I know for certain that he would only enjoy it more if I did. Looking into his eyes, I know there is no hope for me. No one can save me from this evil man.

I will not give him the satisfaction he wants. I will not beg. I will not plead. I came here looking for my sister, and I intend to find her when all of this is over.

"Fuck you," I manage to get out through my clenched teeth.

His eyes gleam at my words. "Oh, a feisty one. I will have so much fun breaking you. Inside and out. I'll take every hole in your body, my cock claiming you. When I'm done, I'll give you to my men to use."

He steps closer to me, and I instinctively try to get away again. I try to crawl away as much as I can being tied up but it's no use. With my ankles and hands bound together, there is no escaping him.

"In the end, you'll wish for death... since it's the only way you'll receive mercy from me."

He grabs a fist full of my hair, his fingers digging painfully into the strands as he pulls me up, forcing me onto my feet, but they won't work. Every muscle in my body is tight, cramped. A loud cry escapes my lips even though I try to swallow it, as the pain of his grip tingles through my scalp.

Without another word, he drags me to the bed and throws me down onto it, making me bounce against the mattress. My body is shaking as I try to roll away to the other side, but it's pointless. He already has a tight grip on my arms, and he's yanking them upward before I even get the chance to move.

I hear something lock into place and before I realize what's happening, my bound hands are attached to the headboard and my bound ankles to the footboard. I'm immobilized. At the mercy of this evil, evil man.

"Mm, look at you…" He runs a finger up my leg, starting at my ankle. He drags it slowly, so slowly it terrifies me. I can't anticipate his next move.

When he reaches my upper thigh, he moves his hand closer to the inside of my leg. Bile rises in my throat when he gets to my barely covered pussy. I clench my jaw and turn my face away from him. I sink deep inside my head, trying to think about anything but the monster touching me.

Still, I feel his touch. Using two fingers, he circles over the most sensitive part of me. Tears spring from my eyes once more. I've never been with a man before. The thought of knowing my first time will be taken from me by this vile bastard sinks deep into my soul. I'll be forever tainted, forever broken.

"Your skin is soft… softer than I expected."

A sob escapes my lips, and I squeeze my eyelids shut. His breath fans against my face. He smells of smoke and whiskey, and I just want to escape this… escape him.

Air fills my lungs, but I refuse to release it. I don't want to smell him. I don't want to feel his fingers on my skin, and yet I know for the rest of my life, I'll never forget this nightmarish moment.

"Open your eyes," he orders. "I want to see the fear in them."

I shake my head. He can take whatever he wants from me. He can use my body however he pleases, but he cannot make me do anything. Nothing.

"Open your fucking eyes, you little bitch." I can feel spit clinging to my face, but I keep my eyes closed anyway. Pain explodes across my cheek, radiating from my jaw and upward. This is my punishment, all for searching for my sister… for wanting to find my only family.

"I'm going to fuck you till you bleed," he growls. His fingers move from my clit, and I hear the sound of him undoing his belt. "I'm going to enjoy your cries, and begging..." I can see the smile on his lips, even with my eyes closed.

"Where is my sister?" If he's going to do this, if he's going to hurt me, then the least he can do is tell me what I came here for. He can give me the answers I desperately seek.

"If she's lucky, she's dead, right where you'll be when I get done with you."

"Please... if you're going to do this..." My heart cracks down the middle, part of my spirit leaking out into this horrible room. "Can you tell me where she is? What will happen to her?"

"You know what... you are right. You should know. She'll be auctioned off to the highest bidder at one of the most prestigious auctions. A place you'd have went had I not wanted a taste of you myself."

Tears sting my eyes. My baby sister will be sold, raped, and passed around by men. She'll be broken, and I'll never get the chance to save her.

"Does that make you sad, Ella?"

I can't stop the tears from escaping my eyes.

"Save your tears for when I'm fucking you. You'll need them if you have any hope of surviving this. In fact, maybe you'll get lucky and I'll like you. I guess it depends on how much you can handle?"

I shake my head, wanting to escape this nightmare so badly, hoping maybe he'll actually shoot me. Certainly, death is better than this. His smile of terror burns into my mind as he reaches for me, spreading my legs wider.

The sound of a door opening fills the room, and I crane my neck in the direction of the noise. Is someone here to save me? To stop this madman from hurting me?

"Boss, I'm sorry to interrupt you, but we're being attacked. If we want to get out of here before they make it inside, we need to leave now," says an unknown man.

I blink my eyes open, seeing my kidnapper snarl with distaste.

"Fucking Christ," the evil bastard mutters, pulling away. "We will just let whoever is coming here for me have fun with you then." He chuckles, and his laughter rains down on me like acid. I twist and turn against the restraints, desperately wanting to break free.

"Bye-bye, Ella." He chuckles and then grips my jaw tightly and kisses me on the mouth harshly. All I want to do is throw up.

His footsteps retreat, each one getting farther and farther away. He is leaving me here, tied up and helpless. If I didn't know any better, I would scream for help, but at this point, I think staying quiet is the best action.

My body shakes like a leaf blowing in the wind as I await my fate. Who could be coming that would scare that man into running?

Someone worse? An even darker monster? The thought sends me into a frenzy. I need to get away, out of this room. I pull on my restraints again, ignoring the sharp pain and the blood that starts trickling down my wrists.

I need to get free. I have to.

Every breath I take is labored. I pull as hard as I can, but the ropes don't budge. My body remains suspended, helpless and ready for the taking. I try and squeeze my legs shut, but it's no use, my muscles are weak, my body exhausted.

Whoever is coming won't have to fight me long to get what they want. The sound of gunshots being fired in the distance and the pounding of heavy footfalls throughout the hallways meet my ears. There are people yelling at each other. I can hear voices, but the door to the room remains closed.

Maybe they won't find me. Maybe I'll be able to escape. If I can't actually break free, maybe I can pretend that I did inside my mind.

The shouting and gunfire ceases and an eerie silence blankets me. I strain to hear anything, a voice, a step... anything at all. Long moments pass, and I pray no one comes.

And then, just like earlier, footsteps break the silence. They're heavy and hold purpose.

No, he came back for me.

I sob uncontrollably, even though I try my hardest to keep the tears in. Part of me wants to plead with him to kill me. I am weak, this I know, but even if I survive this, there is no life worth living after these events.

Between sobs, I notice that the approaching footsteps are accompanied by voices. There are two people coming. Even though I can't make out what they are saying, I know it's not *him*. A tiny sigh of relief escapes me, but when the door opens once more and I see two large men start to approach me, all that is left inside is panic. It grips my soul and holds onto me for dear life.

My entire body tightens when the first man walks right up to me with a wicked smile on his lips.

"Well, well, what do we have here?"

I stare into his dark eyes, trying to find a speck of goodness. He looks just like the other man, but much younger, much more handsome, but in the darkest way possible. He terrifies me, but his presence is nothing compared to the other man's. I can't explain the comparison, and I don't care to.

"Help me. Please, help me," I croak. My voice cracks, and my throat throbs as I speak the words. My plea only widens his smile though, and that terrifies me more. He's not going to let me go. He's going to use me just like the other man. I thrash against the restraints once more, uncaring of the pain that radiates down my arms. Maybe if I'm lucky, the rope will cut into my skin deep enough to slice my wrists.

Maybe I'll die before anything bad can happen. The unknown man reaches for me, and for a split second, I think he is going to untie me, save me. Instead, he just wipes a treacherous tear from my cheek with his finger and brings it to his lips. My lips tremble, and I so badly want to close my eyes again.

His eyes drift closed momentarily, and he looks as if he's lost in some blissful dream. "You do taste rather divine."

No! No! He's going to do the same thing the other man did. He's going to hurt me. My entire body shakes when he takes that same hand and brings it to my chest, his huge hand splaying right between my breasts. I look down to see what he is doing, watching his fingers move.

His dark eyes remain on my face, I can feel the heat of his gaze on my cheeks as he drags two of his fingers down between my breasts and over my belly, leaving a trail of tingling skin behind. I am shocked and confused by my reaction to his touch.

It is warm and less terrifying than the other man's. My thoughts swirl. I must be going insane, losing my mind completely, because I am not revolted by him like I was by the other man. I am still scared beyond disbelief, and my body is shaking, but something deep inside of me knows that this man is the lesser of two evils. He's a monster but nothing compared to the monster I had just witnessed. When his fingers have just about reached my mound, a voice coming from the hall stops his actions.

"Xander, we didn't come here for this." The other voice is laced in annoyance.

I've been so consumed by the presence of this man that I forgot that two guys came in.

"We didn't, but since our father is already gone, don't you think we can at least have some fun? What do you say, little brother? Should we rekindle an old memory?"

Father? Now the resemblance makes sense. I don't know why I didn't see it before. It is so clear now. The dark hair and eyes. The sharp jaw and striking high cheekbones. I tried my best not to look at the other man's face, but the resemblance is too noticeable not to see now.

"We don't have time for this," the other man snaps. "Let's burn this place to the ground. At least he won't have anything to come back to, if he even comes back at all."

"No. Please, don't leave me here. I... I didn't do anything..." My voice erupts like a volcano, the words pouring from my lips. The man touching me eyes me curiously, as if I'm a present he can't wait to open.

"She's right, brother, we can't just leave her here." A smirk filled with pleasure pulls at the man's lips. I blink, fear tumbling out of control inside of me as I wait for him to say something else. "Maybe we can bring her with us. Torture the truth out of her. I know the perfect method." At that very moment, he moves his hand, his fingers pressing harshly against my mound. I gasp and cry out in pain, fighting against the restraints. I feel warm blood sliding down my arms, the warmth of it over my skin strangely soothing.

"Xander..." The other man's footsteps fill the room. His tone is impatient, and I wonder if I could reason with him. If he'd release me instead.

"P-please..." I beg, and more tears fall. The other man comes into view. His eyes are on me, but his gaze wavers, guilt consuming his features.

"She's his type. Sweet. Blonde, with big blue eyes." The man named Xander snickers. "I bet he kept this one for a while. She must know something. I could break her, snap her in two, send her body in pieces to him."

His words strike fear deep down in my belly, a different kind of fear.... An all-consuming fear. This man doesn't just plan to break me, to rape me; he plans to kill me and use my body for revenge.

"I... I don't know him..." I shake my head, trying to get them to understand. "I..." The pain in my wrists consumes me, and I feel my arms growing heavy.

"Xander, you need to make up your mind. Bring her with us, I don't give a fuck, but I am burning this place and all the dead bodies inside of it to the ground," the other man says, but it sounds so far away. I can't really explain what is happening... I can hear my pulse pounding in my ears, and my vision starts to blur.

No, I can't die like this. I can't. I won't.

I thrash against the bed but feel nothing, not even pain. Why don't I feel anything?

Darkness closes in around me, and I know then that I am about to pass out. The two men loom above me. The man named Xander still has his hands on my body; his hand is warm, and I want to sink into it, into the warmth it brings.

As my eyes drift closed, pain is still absent for the moment. My last thought before everything goes completely black is to wonder if I am ever going to wake up again.

And if I do, what does fate have in store for me?

2

ander

I PULL the knife from my boot and slash the rope holding her wrists and her ankles together. Thank fucking god she is passed out, and I don't have to deal with her struggling. It'd be worse for her if she was awake. My patience is far too thin to be dealing with my father's whores.

My gaze sweeps over her nearly naked body. My mind is already filled with all the wonderful things I'm going to do to her. Father dressed her in nothing more than scraps, yet another trait of his whores. She definitely belongs to him. Too bad. I would have enjoyed fucking her, but I won't knowing she has been with him.

I can't deny her beauty though. Strawberry-blonde hair frames her heart-shaped face, and her pink full lips are kissable. She's got big blue doe eyes that I imagine looking up at me while I force my cock between her lips.

She's everything a man could want when fucking, but again, I won't touch her knowing my father has. Pushing the thoughts aside since that's not what I am taking her for, I slide my arms under her body and lift her to my chest. She doesn't weigh hardly anything, and I can carry her with ease. For some reason, I don't fucking like the thought.

She should eat some fucking food, put some meat on her bones or something.

I walk out the door past Damon, who is shaking his head at me. He's disappointed, angry with my choice to bring her instead of just let her go. Good thing I don't need his approval... or anyone else's for that matter. There's a reason I'm the leader of the Rossi empire, and he is not.

I get the fucking hard shit done, the shit no one else wants to do because it crosses lines no one wants to talk about.

I've killed women. I've beaten women. Am I proud of it? Of course not. But I do what I have to fucking do. My family and my ability as a leader are defined by the choices I make. If I can't do something, then I cannot expect my men to do it either.

"I don't like this, Xander. You don't know if she's telling the truth or not. She looked pretty fucking scared to just be one of his random whores," Damon rambles, as he douses the house in gasoline.

"I don't really care what you think, Damon. I'm taking her. You burn the house down, and that'll be the end of it. Maybe next time, we'll actually catch him," I snap, too annoyed to deal with his moral code of bullshit.

I pick up my pace, walking down the hall and away from Damon. If I wanted my brother's input, I would ask for it. My eyes move over the contents of this place. It's just a fucking mansion, full of valuables.

That only angers me more. He didn't leave any fucking clues, no papers, not a trace of anything. The only reason we knew he was here was because of a now-dead guard we had tortured the info out of. He'd been a long-time friend of the family and was responsible for disposing of my father's body, which he clearly didn't do, since the bastard is still alive.

With my anger threatening to boil to the surface, I tighten my hold on the small body in my arms, drawing a faint whimper from her lips. I look down at her beautiful face, so peaceful looking, now that she is passed out. Her long amber-colored lashes fan against her cheek. There's a slight bruising below her right eye, the skin black and blue as if she'd been slapped. Something about that angers me as well, and I don't know why. I've laid my hands on countless women, and in much worse ways than that, and yet, a slight bruising of this woman's face has me feeling some strange emotions.

I walk out the front door, down the steps, and into the driveway. The unnamed woman bounces in my arms every step I take, and I hold her tighter. Her head presses against my shoulder like she is leaning into me for comfort, for protection. It awakens an odd feeling inside of me. A feeling that surprisingly tamps my anger down... I don't like it, but then again, it's not an unsettling feeling either.

I walk up to the SUV where two of my men are already waiting. They look at the girl in my arms and then back up to me. They know better than to ask questions. I motion for them to open the back door and when they do, I slide into the back seat, still holding her in my arms. I could probably let her go now, place her down on the leather seats, but I like the feeling of her in my arms.

Startled by the thought, I curl my fingers into her skin, feeling the heat. I imagine her whimper in pain as I do, and that thought makes my cock hard.

"Where to?" the driver asks from the front seat, interrupting my thoughts.

"Home."

He doesn't hesitate when I answer, and we drive off the property as if we just came for a short visit, instead of a killing spree. I spend the majority of the ride to the mansion looking at her. Studying her features... wondering what she looks like when she smiles.

What a ridiculous thought. *Smiling.* No one does that in my presence. I try to imagine myself torturing her, breaking her bones, slicing her skin. For the first time ever, the thought revolts me, but I know I don't have a choice.

I need to protect my family, my son, above all. The things she may know, the secrets, they're all that matters. Finding my father and killing him, that's the important thing here, and if torturing her gives me those answers then that's what I'll do.

The car comes to a halt, and I am about to ask the driver why the hell we are stopped when I look up and realize we are already home. *What the fuck!* I must have gotten lost just staring at her like an idiot. I shake my head at my own stupidity. I need to stop this nonsense, and I need to stop it now. There is no room for feelings in my life.

My son. My family, they're all that matters.

Not some woman my father probably dipped his dick into half a dozen times. She's nothing, no one, and the sooner I see her as that, the easier this will all be. I get out of the car, with her body still in my arms, and walk up to the front door. One of guards is already holding the door open for me, so I walk in. I head for the staircase leading up to the bedrooms when I stop myself. My feet stop dead in their tracks.

What the fuck am I doing?

I can't bring her up here. I can't have her around my son. I can't treat her like a guest in my house. I can't do any of these fucking things because she is the fucking enemy. Curling my fingers into her tender flesh, I clench my jaw and turn on my heels, walking down the stairs and into the basement.

I carry her into one of the holding cells that hasn't been used since my son was born. It's cold and damp, and it doesn't seem right to leave her down here. Deep in the pit of my stomach, I feel that this is wrong. But that's merely my infatuation with her, or at least that's what I tell myself. I lay her small body down on the cot. When I do this, I realize one of her small hands is fisting into my shirt, as if she is trying to hold onto me.

I peel her fingers away and watch her sleeping features turn into a frown. It's strange how she was so fearful while awake, but now she clings to me as if I'm her savior. I almost laugh at the thought. She has no idea the things I can and will do to get what I want.

I stand up straight and watch her barely dressed body curl up into herself like she is cold. There are no blankets down here. Comfort has never been on my mind when it comes to holding a prisoner, and I know it shouldn't be any other way with her either, but it is.

I briefly think about tying her up in my bedroom, but her wrists and ankles are already so bloody it will only cause more damage. I have to leave her here; it's the right thing to do.

She is the enemy... a foe, my father's whore. Repeating the verse over and over again inside my head, I force my feet to move, taking me out of the room. I close the door and lock it behind me. I have to do what's obligated of me.

I need to think about my son, and his future, about his safety, not some woman who's only useful for the hole between her legs. I don't have room for a woman in my life. After all, the last one ended up dead because of her own stupidity. She proved to me that you can't trust anyone, no one but yourself. Still, I look at this fucking woman and feel a thud in my chest.

My heart is beating hard and fast because of her, and I don't fucking understand why. I wrap my hand around one of the iron bars, envisioning myself wrapping that same hand around her delicate throat.

Would I squeeze hard enough to kill her? Or would I test the limits, showing her what would happen if she disobeyed me?

It doesn't matter even if she is an innocent in all of this. If she doesn't tell me what I want to know, she'll pay just like everyone else... with her blood.

3

lla

My eyes feel as if there are elephants sitting on them. They're impossibly heavy, and I use every ounce of strength possible to open them. As soon as I do, I remember that what I thought was nothing more than a nightmare is actually my reality. A shiver runs down my spine. Partly out of fear, partly because I'm actually freezing.

It takes me a moment to take in my surroundings. I'm on a cot, in some kind of cell, but that is not the scariest part. It's the man who is standing next to my cot looming over me that has my heart rate skipping a beat.

"Good morning, little mouse." His voice is deep; his dark eyes hold me in place.

He takes a seat on the way-too-small cot beside me and, for a moment, I think his weight is going to break the thing beneath us. He's a big man, rippling muscles, at least a foot taller than me.

His leg is touching my ribs, and I want to move away from him, but his body heat is just too precious to refuse. Instead of pulling away, I move closer.

"Why am I here?" My voice is small and weak, and my throat and my mouth feel like they have cotton balls shoved in them. I could really use a drink of water, but I'm not dumb enough to ask this man for anything.

"You don't get to ask questions. I do and you are going to answer every single one of them or I'm going to have to do some things you don't want me to do." The warning is clear. If I don't give him the answers he wants, whatever they might be, he will hurt me.

I try and conjure up a response. I don't know what kind of information he thinks I have for him, because I know nothing.

"Where is my father now?" There's no emotion to his features... in fact, he looks more like a statue than a man.

"I don't know. I didn't even know he was your father until you showed up. I don't even know his name."

"You are lying. You are one of his whores; you must know something. You cannot expect me to believe a single word you say when you're dressed the way you are."

I shake my head gently. "I'm not lying, and I'm not a whore." My cheeks heat slightly at the words. I would never wear something like this by choice. I've never even slept with a man before

"Really?" His voice is bitter, and his eyes turn violent. I don't even get a chance to respond to him before he has me by the hair, his huge hand and thick fingers digging painfully into my scalp.

"Please, Xander..." His name falls from my lips, and I realize as soon as I've said it that I've made a mistake.

He pulls me into his face, a darkness surges to the surface, and I feel like I might puke. With his hand in my hair, I can't escape him. I whimper, pain radiating across my scalp.

"Don't try and humanize me. I'll kill you without even blinking." His other hand comes into view, the fingers flexing as he wraps them around my throat.

Panic floods my system, and I instinctively start to fight back. My arms strike out, hitting him, and my nails dig into his skin, scratching him, but my attack does nothing to him. He just laughs at my feeble attempts and tightens his grip on my throat. He pulls me really close to him, so that his face is right next to mine. I can smell him, spice and danger; it tickles my nose.

"I'm going to give you one more chance. Before I really start to hurt you, and this isn't some attempt. I will hurt you."

He lets go of my throat, and I slump back down to the cot like a rag doll, gasping for air. My lungs can't fill with air fast enough.

"Tell me what you know and where my father is." His voice is clipped and angry. I know he is losing his patience with me, but there is nothing I can tell him that is going to make him believe me.

"I don't know." I put every ounce of emotion into my words, hoping that he can see my honesty. "I've never even seen your father until today. I don't know his name. Let alone where he is or where he is going to be. I don't know him. I swear." I feel like I'm in front of a jury trying to convince them of my innocence... Xander being the judge and the executioner.

Disappointment flickers in Xander's dark gaze. "It's really a shame that my father had you before. I would have loved to fuck you raw. Fuck the defiance right out of you."

Anger gets a hold of me, and I find a sudden ounce of courage. "For the last time, your father didn't have me... No one has had me." I don't know why I added the last part, but I regret it as soon as it's left my lips.

Xander smirks. "You are trying to tell me than no one has been here before." His hand is suddenly between my legs, grabbing me there harshly. I gasp and try to move away but his other hand moves to my shoulder, holding me in place before I can move an inch.

He leans into me, so his mouth is right by my ear. "So... you're telling me that if I slide my finger inside you, it's going to be tight like a virgin pussy?"

His words make my whole body shiver. Partly because of fear and partly because some sick part of me wonders what his fingers inside me would feel like.

Would I like it? Would he make me come? The questions swirl around inside my head, and I quickly shove them away to concentrate on the danger before me. I try and digest everything he's said.

If this is all it would take to prove to him that I'm not his father's whore, then I would definitely let him finger me. Maybe once he discovers the truth, he'll let me go. He'll realize I'm innocent and not the enemy.

"If I let you finger me, will you believe me and let me go?"

"If you let me?" He laughs without a trace of humor. "My little mouse, don't you understand yet that I'll do whatever I want to your body. You're my property now. Your body is mine to do with, however I please."

"Fine then, finger me so you have your answer since you don't believe a single word I'm saying." I barely finish saying the words when I feel him shove my panties to the side and his fingers slip between my folds to find my entrance.

Panic makes my body go stiff. I grip onto his forearm. The muscles quiver beneath my fingers. I don't know why I grabbed onto his arm, maybe to stop him? To feel some type of control over the situation? I don't know. My thighs squeeze together.

"Spread your legs," he orders

I try to relax my legs. I squeeze my eyes shut, hoping it won't hurt too bad. Never having done this before, I don't know what to expect.

"Please go slow," I whisper, not knowing if he even heard me or if he would care enough to do it at all.

I feel his fingertip slip in as if he is probing me. Slowly, he pushes his thick finger inside. I can feel my walls gripping his finger tightly as he pushes in to his knuckle and then even farther until he is in all the way.

I gasp and my back arches off the cot slightly at the foreign sensation. It doesn't hurt, not like I'd expected.

His finger feels so thick inside of me, and I can't imagine what it would feel like to have his cock inside me instead. The thought ignites something deep inside my core.

"Look at me." His voice is different. For the first time today, he doesn't sound so angry. I follow his command and pry my eyes open. His face is only a few inches from mine, looking at me like he is trying to solve a puzzle and all the answers lie somewhere within my face. I use the time to inspect his features in return. Of course, he is annoyingly handsome. Dark alluring eyes, strong jaw line, and full lips that are begging to be kissed. His hair is dark and disheveled. He looks tired... so tired.

We stare at each other for a few moments, and I forget that he still has a finger inside of me until he pulls it out. I feel empty and cold when he does, and both of those feelings confuse the hell out of me. I shouldn't be feeling this way about this man.

"How did you end up at my father's place?" he questions.

"I don't know. I just woke up there... dressed in this." I look down at the lingerie barely covering my body.

He nods as if he actually believes what I say. Then he straightens, stands up, and turns like he is about to leave.

Strangely, I don't want him to go. For the first time in hours, I feel safe, even though I know it's a temporary feeling. There is nothing safe about Xander. Nothing at all.

"Can I go now?"

"Don't be ridiculous." He steps out of the cell and closes the door behind him. Betrayal hits me hard. I thought he believed me... how stupid could I be?

"Don't leave me in here." I wrap my arms around myself, suddenly realizing how cold it is down here, at the loss of his body heat. "I'm freezing."

"Maybe if I find time later, I'll bring you a blanket. If not, I'll see you in the morning and we can talk more then."

I jump up from the cot, anger suddenly flooding my body. "Why are you keeping me here? I told you I don't know anything. You felt for yourself that I'm not one of your father's whores."

"You think simply because you have a tight pussy that you can fool me into believing you're a virgin?" He scowls as if I've insulted him or something.

"I'm not lying to you. I swear!" I grip onto the cold bars, willing him to believe me.

"We'll see, until then, I think I'll keep you to play with, just for a little bit." His words make me stumble backward, and I almost fall on my ass. Why did I believe he would let me go? "Goodnight, little mouse." He grins before disappearing into the dark hallway.

The cold seems to seep deeper into my bones as he walks away. My body shivers uncontrollably, my teeth clicking together. I sit back down on the cot and pull my knees to my chest. I try and force myself to go to sleep but it's so cold there's no way sleep will come.

I look down at my hands. My wrists are still bloody, my face aches, and a distinct pounding forms behind my eyes.

Tears well in my eyes. I've cried so much today that I don't want to cry anymore. I tuck my chin into my chest, trying to stay warm. I should be grateful, right? I'm alive and Xander hasn't hurt me. Not really. He saved me from all the things his father would have done to me. Xander is definitely worth fearing, but the way he looks at me with the interest that appears in his eyes... I know I'm more valuable to him alive than dead, and I am going to use that fact to survive.

How the hell did I end up in this situation? All I wanted to do is find my sister... I still do. She's only just turned eighteen, and she's never been on her own. She needs me. I've been her legal guardian since she was sixteen, and our parents died driving home drunk from an all-night binger. I was only nineteen at the time myself, but what other choice did I have? I couldn't let her go into foster care. She's the only family I have left, so I replaced our parents. Worked my ass off to support us. Sacrificed my social life completely by taking care of her... and I would do it over again a million times if I had to. She's my everything, and now I've failed her so fucking much.

I exhale all the air in my lungs, clenching my fists together. I look at my surroundings. There is no escaping this cell. Then I realize something. When Xander left, he didn't lock me inside. I didn't hear a lock, and I didn't see a key. Though it's not unlikely that the door locked by itself when it closed. I shove my fists into my eyes. How could I get myself into such a mess?

I remove my hands and stare at the door of the cell. Xander's not a dumb man, and I doubt he'd make it that easy for me to escape. Yet, it doesn't hurt me to check. I get up from the cot on shaky legs and walk over to the door. The coldness on my feet makes me yelp but I bite my lip, stifling the noise.

If I'm going to escape, I'll need to be as quiet as a mouse. The irony of the statement makes me smile, and it feels foreign as I do so. I haven't smiled in days, it seems. Not since I came to that house to rescue my sister and got myself here.

Focusing on the task at hand, I push and pull on the door, the cold bars beneath my fingers making me shiver more. I'm cold, so damn cold, and I just want out of this godforsaken room. I clench my jaw, ignoring the shivers that rack my body and put more effort into moving the door, but it doesn't budge. It's solid as a brick wall.

I lean down and examine the lock instead... it'd be easy to pick, if I had something to pick it with, that is. Shaking my head in defeat, I walk back toward the cot. I slump down and huddle into the fetal position. I stay like this for a long time, could be hours, days, I don't really know. What I do know is that eventually my eyes grow heavy with exhaustion, and I slip into a fitful sleep, wondering what Xander plans to do with me next.

4

ander

I PACE the floor of my bedroom; my fingers sink into my hair as I grip it almost painfully. I feel conflicted... confused. I've never felt this way about a prisoner and definitely not about a woman before. I don't want to hurt her... I really fucking don't. But I have an image to uphold, a duty, a job as the boss of the family.

There are people relying on me, people who need me.

People like my son.

I grit my teeth and exhale out of my nostrils. Maybe I just need to fuck her out of my system, get a taste of her. My mind drifts back to the memory of the way her tight pussy clenched around my finger. How she claimed to be a virgin and clammed up at my touch. She did feel like a virgin but that's no proof.

I'm trapped between two scenarios, and I can't figure out which one is the truth. Maybe she's a good actress? Or maybe she is telling the truth? Though I find it hard to believe such an attractive woman could still be intact, it wouldn't be completely impossible.

I clench my jaw tighter. Her pussy felt like heaven wrapped around my finger and since coming back upstairs, I've done everything humanly possible next to cutting my own legs off to stop myself from going back down there.

She looks so fragile, like a delicate fucking flower, and I don't want to snuff out the light that she needs to grow, but I can't just let her go either. I need whatever information she knows... she must know something more. Innocent or not, if she can't tell me anything then she has no use in my house, and if there is no use for her then she might as well be dead.

I leave my room in a huff and head back toward the basement, my feet moving all on their own. Emotions I've never felt before swirl deep inside my head. What is it about this strawberry-blonde woman that tugs at my fucking heartstrings?

She's under my skin, inside my head, and wreaking havoc on my life, and she's been here what, a few hours' time? I can't let this continue... I'm stronger than this. Caring for her, that's a complete weakness.

I rush down the stairs faster, this weird feeling in my gut taking root. Something is off. I reach for my gun just to make sure it's there even though I know it's always there. Old habits never die, I suppose.

When I enter the basement, the sinking feeling I had is confirmed. A male voice echoes through the dark hallway, his shadow lingering along the walls.

Anger rears its ugly head, and I know I'm about to do something that I may not like.

I reach for my gun again, this time taking it out. I flick the safety off, holding it in front of me, ready to shoot at any given time. I start to walk around the corner when I spot one of my newest guards in front of *her* cell, trying to unlock the door.

I grit my teeth. What the fuck is this prick doing? I told every single one of my guys to stay out of the basement. He knew I was hiding something, but was it any of his fucking business to investigate? No.

The fury festering inside me boils over when I hear the cell unlock, and I watch him step into the cell. "Now let's have some fun before the boss comes back. Spread those creamy white thighs for me. I want to see if you're as innocent as you look."

As quietly as I can, I move closer until I'm right behind him.

I don't dare look at the girl's face. I don't want to see the spiraling fear inside her baby-blue eyes, not unless I put it there. Raising my gun to the idiot's head, I pull the trigger. His body hits the floor before the sound of the gun going off has even reached my ears.

A scream from my sweet mouse fills my ears.

She needs me... she needs my protection.

The thought forms in my mind and I ignore it.

I step over the dead body and into the cell. I'll have to get one of the other men to clean this up, and then I'll have to call a meeting letting everyone know that no one touches her. No one. My eyes scan the cell, until they find her tiny body. She is huddled up on the floor against the wall farthest away, looking just as scared as I thought she would be.

Like a mouse caught in a trap, she is at my mercy. I stare at her for a long moment, wondering what I will do with her. There's a feral look in her eyes, and I wonder if she thinks I'm going to hurt her? The muscle in my chest beats harshly.

Guilt washes over me... a feeling I rarely experience anymore. I don't know why I feel bad for her, why I feel bad for killing this bastard in her presence. I shouldn't feel anything for her at all... I shouldn't care at all about anything that pertains to her, but I do.

"Come on, let's get you cleaned up." I gesture for her to come forward, but she doesn't move or give me any other sign that she heard what I said.

She just keeps staring at the body lying on the floor outside the cell. Yet, another indicator that she is telling the truth. How she could have been one of my father's whores and get spooked by a man being shot in the head?

Shaking my head at the thought, I walk deeper into the cell, stopping only once I'm standing right in front of her. The tip of my shoes almost touch her toe.

"Are you coming?" I try my best to keep my tone soft. She's already scared enough as it is, what's the point in scaring her more?

Still nothing. No reaction at all.

I eye her once more. Her body is tucked into itself as if to make her already small body appear smaller. Her fingers grip her knees so hard her knuckles turn white. I inspect her features closer; they're a cross between fear and shock.

She's definitely never witnessed a murder, or any crime, before. Fuck, she's going to be a piece of work, and I just don't have the time for that shit.

But you want to.

I sigh loudly and stick the gun back into the holster at my side. Then I kneel down beside her and slide my arms under her small body. I lift her up in my arms, and I wonder if she will fight me or beg me to put her down. When she doesn't, I wonder if she's had a mental breakdown.

As I bring her body into my chest, she goes stiff and rigid at first, but once I stand up and start walking with her, her arms snake around my neck. She cuddles into my chest, like I'm the only person who can protect her from the monsters in the dark. She hasn't realized yet that I *am* the monster in the dark.

Who does she think I am? I should probably just put her back in that cell and lock the door. It's what I'd do with any other person... right? *Wrong.* Any other person would be dead by now.

Frustration over this tiny woman spirals out of control inside me. I should stop this whole thing before it gets even further... I really should. But she just feels too fucking perfect in my arms, and I imagine her in my bed, my cock sliding deep inside her, my name falling from her lips. The urge to toss her to the floor consumes me, and I tighten my hold on her instead. I'm fighting myself tooth and nail over her, and I don't even know why.

"You... you killed him?" she finally says.

"Yeah? What's your point?" I try my hardest not to sound angry, but I am. I'm so fucking angry, at her, at myself, at everything.

"W... why did you kill him?" Her voice is fragile, matching her delicate facial features. She's so tiny I could crush her in an instant. I could wrap my hands around her throat and remove her existence from my life... and I fucking don't.

"I don't fucking know," I growl, reaching the bedroom... *my* bedroom. I kick the half open door all the way open and walk inside. Cradling her body against mine feels wrong, and right, and still so fucking wrong. I walk over to the king-sized bed and toss her down onto the mattress. She scurries backward, away from me.

Her doe eyes dazzle with fear.

"What are you going to do to me?" Her bottom lip trembles as she speaks.

God, she's so gorgeous when she's on the verge of tears.

"I don't know, Mouse." I pause briefly, scrubbing a hand down my face. "Part of me wants to put a bullet in your head; another part wants to fuck you senseless."

I see her thighs clench together at my response, and I wonder if she would like me fucking her. I wouldn't be gentle like she most likely deserves... I'd be ruthless, sinister. I'd fuck her until she was screaming for me to stop, and even then, I'd still keep going.

I shake the thought away, and when she doesn't respond, I walk over to the dresser and grab a shirt out for her, flinging it at her over my shoulder.

"Either way, you should probably be scared, Mouse. I don't take mercy on anyone, whether that be in bed or out of bed. There's a chance I might fuck you and kill you moments later."

When I turn around, I find her face a mask of horror. She's scared, and that's exactly what I need her to be for this to work out. If she's scared of me, it'll make it easier for me to kill her once I get her out of my system.

"Go shower and make sure you clean your wounds well. I don't want you to die *before* I'm done with you."

I remain standing, watching her movements as she slowly gets up from the bed, those big blue eyes of hers never leaving mine. When her bare feet hit the floor, she darts toward one of the open doors to her right. I haven't told her which room is the bathroom and yet she finds it without thought.

She escapes inside with the shirt, *my* shirt, in her hand, and I exhale, clenching my jaw so hard I can feel my molars grind together.

I need a drink... a strong one. I also need to kill her, but I don't think I can do it. I pull my gun from its holster and examine it. All I have to do is lift the barrel and pull the trigger. All I have to do is pull the fucking trigger... but I won't. I can't. Why? I don't fucking know. I never had this issue before.

I hear the water in the bathroom turn on. An image of her completely naked beneath the spray enters my mind. I shake my head as if doing so will remove the image from my mind, but it doesn't.

Why is she under my skin? In my head?

Normally, I wouldn't have to rationalize with myself over killing someone, but with her, I have to and I don't like it. I don't like the power she holds over me for not being able to do it.

I walk over to the small bar I have in the corner of the room and grab a bottle of bourbon, as well as a glass. I consider drinking the entire fucking thing, but that wouldn't be smart. I need to be sober, or somewhat sober, in case there is an attack.

So, instead, I pour half a glass and walk back over to the bed, swirling the amber liquid around. I sit on the edge of the bed and wait for her to finish her shower, contemplating my next move. My gun sits heavily against my thigh.

When I hear the water shut off, I down what's left of the bourbon, letting the warmth of the liquid give me the courage I need to finish the job.

Will you live or die to today, Mouse?

5

*E*lla

I step out of the luxurious shower and wrap myself up in one of the fluffy towels hanging from a rack. I take my time drying off, all well wondering what I should expect when I step out of this bathroom. My body is still shaking, from fear or cold I don't know really.

Could be either or both at this point. I start to dry my hair and play his words inside my head. He said it's either sex or death... and somehow, I doubt he wanted me to get clean so he could kill me. On the other hand, he gave me a t-shirt.

His t-shirt. I shake my head, confusion over his words coursing through my body.

Why would he want me to cover up if he wanted to fuck me? Maybe he is just saying these things to keep me scared? But he did kill one of his men for me, so obviously, he doesn't want anyone else to have me? But he also said he may kill me, even after having sex with me. I'm so confused by him. Everything he says and does is a contradiction, but my gut tells me that he won't kill me.

I eye myself in the mirror for a moment. The bruise on my cheek isn't nearly as bad as I'd have expected it to be. The hit itself hurt more than the actual bruise looks.

My wrists throb, but the pain is a great reminder that I'm alive, at least for now. My gaze moves over to the bathroom door. I know I can't hide out in this bathroom forever, no matter how badly I want to, and something tells me that the longer I take in here, the angrier he is going to get out there. And if he's angry, he's less likely to bargain, and if I want to make it out of this alive, I'm going to have bargain every single thing I've got.

I take the plain cotton t-shirt and slip it on. The material is soft, and I relish in the warmth it provides me. My gaze slips down to the discarded lingerie on the floor. I want to burn them, rip them to shreds, but instead, I pick them up and toss them into the trash can. I don't care that I don't have any panties. I'd rather be completely exposed then put those disgraceful things back on.

I walk slowly over to the door, pulling at the hem of the t-shirt. It rests just above my knees, confirming just how much bigger Xander is than I, but still, it's not long enough. Twisting the door knob, I walk out into the dark bedroom.

It takes a moment for my eyes to adjust to the lighting but when they do, I notice Xander sitting on the very edge of the bed. The first thing I notice is the gun lying next to him. I think about running back inside the bathroom, but what good would that do me?

He'd just follow me and shoot me anyway, and as badly as I want to run, running will not get me out of this situation.

Gathering all the courage I have left in me, I walk up to him until my bare legs are almost touching his covered ones.

"What now?"

"Give me a reason not to kill you, Mouse. One single fucking reason. If you can't give me information, then offer me something else that will make me want to keep you."

My eyes widen as he picks the gun up. He doesn't point it at me, but it's still a threat looming between us. I know it would only take a second for him to raise it and pull the trigger.

"I would tell you if I knew anything... I would help you catch your father if I could, but I swear I don't know anything. I can't give you any information when there is none to give. I don't have money or anything else to offer you. All I have is myself... that's all I can give you. Me... if that's what you want. I'll give you me, if it's the only form of payment I can give you in return for letting me go."

My heart races, slamming against my ribcage painfully. I can't believe I just said what I did. I just offered myself to this man who already told me that he's either going to hurt me or kill me, but for some reason, I can't believe he would do the latter. Xander's dark eyes meet my frightened ones. There's a curiosity in his gaze as it flicks over my body. I can practically see what he is thinking, and the thoughts make me shiver.

What's the worst he can do to me? Take my virginity. Degrade me. Hurt me. But when it's all over, I'll still be alive, and that's all that matters, right? I'll be able to find my sister.

"I won't be gentle with you, and I cannot even guarantee that I won't put a bullet in your head when I'm done with you." He says the words as if he is talking more to himself than me.

I swallow around the knot in my throat, knowing that bargaining with the devil before me will do me no good, and yet still, I say the words that sit against the tip of my tongue. "I... I'm giving myself to you. All I want is to live... to walk away from this all when it's over. That's it."

"Why would I value you giving yourself to me if I could just take you by force and there is nothing you could do about it?" A wicked grin paints his face, and I swallow hard. Not really having a good answer to that, I just shrug, knowing that he is right. If he wanted to, he could overpower me easily.

"Why were you at my father's house?" His eyes burni right through me, holding me in place.

"I was looking for my sister. She's been missing for weeks and some people told me that she was at this night club. So, I went there, showing everybody her picture. I didn't find her. I was just about to give up, turn around and leave, but some men grabbed me before I could. I asked them about her, but they just ignored me. They drugged me, I think..."

I sigh, remembering bits and pieces that flickered through my mind. "I don't really remember everything that happened. One minute, I was awake, and the next, I wasn't. Then I woke up in the bedroom. I was on the floor with my hands and feet bound together. I don't know how I got to the room or who put me in the lingerie. I wasn't awake for any of that."

"How did you get onto the bed?" Xander's face is void of all emotion.

My body revolts just thinking about our little encounter. "Your father came into the room and put me on the bed."

"Did he touch you?" His question twists a knife deep into my heart. Tears instantly fill my eyes. I don't want to appear weak to Xander, but I'll never forget the things his father said to me, or the way his hands felt on my skin.

"He told me what he was going to do to me and then he started... touching me." The bile rises in my throat, burning up every inch of my esophagus. "But he got interrupted by a guard coming in... he said that the house was under attack. They left without saying another word to me."

Through my tears, I look up at Xander and see some flicker of emotion in his eyes. It looks a lot like pity. I usually don't like to have anyone pity me, but with a man like him, I'll take any emotion I can get.

"I tried to get free, but the ropes were too tight. They cut into my skin, and that's why these cuts are so deep." I look down at my messed-up wrists, wishing the wounds would heal already. "Then you came in the room and found me."

He nods, as if for the first time today, he actually believes everything I'm saying. A memory dislodges from my mind... right then.

"Wait... your father said something to me about an auction." I lift my gaze to Xander's. He looks indifferent. "I asked him where my sister was, and he said, 'one of the most prestigious auctions,' whatever that means. He didn't give me a location or even tell me when it is. But if my sister is in danger, then I need to save her and maybe you can find your father in the process."

"There's no saving your sister, Mouse, and my father is not stupid enough to be anywhere near that auction."

"Xander, I have to save her," I plead, hoping that it's okay to call him by his name now.

"No, Mouse, you don't. If she is lucky, she'll die before she's sold to anyone."

I don't believe him. I cannot. I'll find a way out. I'll survive.

"As for our agreement, I can't promise you anything." He exhales a ragged breath.

I can see the conflict in his eyes. "The things I'm guessing my father told you he'd do to you, I'll most likely end up doing. I'm not a good man, Mouse. I don't treasure things, and I care for no one. And just because I fuck you, it doesn't mean you'll make it out of this alive."

My chest heaves; panic grips me. I want to run so badly my legs beg me onward, but my brain... my brain tells me to stay in place. He thinks he is like his father, but I know better. I may be naive but I'm not stupid. He wouldn't do the things his father threatened me with.

"I'll be whatever you want me to be. Just please... don't kill me. Let me go so I can try to find my sister." I drop my gaze down to my hands in front of me. I feel weak begging, but what else is there to do? After all of this, I just wish to come out alive, and to eventually find my baby sister.

"Get on your knees," he orders, and my eyes snap up to his instantly.

"Wh-what?" I stutter.

"Get. On. Your. Knees." He enunciates every single word through his teeth, and I follow his directions, dropping to the floor. My knees land, and sweat starts to form on my hands. I'm terrified, and my stomach tightens with the unknown. Xander moves from the bed, coming to stand directly in front of me. His large frame is intimidating, and I have to stop myself from backpedaling.

He peers down at me, a smirk that would scare even the devil appearing on his lips. "You want to live, Mouse? Then you need to prove to me your worthiness. Give me a reason to keep you around for a bit."

I gulp and nod in understanding as he reaches for the belt of his expensive suit. Panic stirs inside me, but I tamp it down, knowing it's either this or death.

"Have you ever sucked a cock? Ever been choked by one?" He undoes his belt, flicking the button on his pants. I see a sliver of toned flesh as his pants hang low against his hips. I clench my thighs together at the feelings surging through me.

Lust. Desire. Two emotions I've never felt even once in my life.

I shake my head, my cheeks heating with embarrassment at his questions. Taking one of his large hands, he reaches for my face, tucking some still wet hair behind my ear. The simple touch is somehow comforting in all of this, and I have to fight the urge to lean into his hand.

"You really are an innocent little mouse." His hand ghosts down my face until he reaches my chin. Holding it between his thumb and his index finger, he tilts my face upward.

"Open your mouth," he orders, and I obey without hesitation. "No teeth, just your tongue, your lips, and your hands." I try and nod but his grip on my chin is firm, reminding me has all the control now.

With his other hand, he unzips his zipper and his pants fall the floor. My eyes widen at the very large, very scary penis pointed directly at me.

"If you bite me, I will kill you. Now don't act so frightened and get to sucking."

I exhale sharply. Instead of forcing my head onto his cock like I thought he would, he lets go of my chin and waits for me to act.

I gulp down all the fear running rampant throughout my body and lean forward. Opening my mouth real wide, I stick out my tongue and take the tip of his penis into my mouth. It's warm and much smoother than I thought it would be.

I close my lips around him and swirl my tongue, testing the feeling. I peek up at him, trying to gauge his reaction but his eyes are closed like he is concentrating really hard on not losing control. I try to move down, taking more of him inside of my mouth.

I take more, as far as I can until my gag reflex kicks in. I panic, realizing I still don't have even half of him inside my mouth. Then I remember he said I can use my hands as well. While continuing to suck on the upper part of his penis, I wrap my small shaky hand around the base of his shaft and squeeze it gently.

For a moment, I wonder if I am doing this right? Xander hasn't complained yet, nor has he moved, and his eyes remain shut, his body like a statue.

What if he isn't enjoying it? What if this is my one chance to show him why he shouldn't kill me?

Realizing just how true my fears might be, I stroke him up and down... synchronizing my hand with how I take him into my mouth. I make sure every inch of his cock gets pleasure and when I feel him flex inside my grip and an almost inaudible grunt escapes his lips, I assume I'm doing something right.

Knowing this makes me feel like I have all the power... which is ridiculous since I'm the one on my knees, pleasing him. But it gives me the ego boost I need to continue.

I tighten my grip just a little and pick up the pace. I feel him flex his hips again and taste a small amount of saltiness on my tongue. I continue sucking and stroking him, putting my all into every single suck and stroke. My jaw starts to ache, and my knees dig painfully into the floor, but I don't care. I peek up at him again... and this time, I'm surprised to find his eyes are open.

He reaches out and cradles the side of my face, as if to comfort me. Just as I feel him flex a final time inside of my mouth, his whole body goes tense, a groan of pleasure escapes his lips, and his eyes close momentarily. I stare up at him, watching the blissful moment take place, wishing he always looked as peaceful as he does right now.

Hot salty liquid fills my mouth, and I instinctively swallow it. It doesn't taste bad, but it's not pleasant either. I release him from my mouth with a loud pop that echoes through the room. My cheeks flame red when I realize I've just made a man come for the first time.

"It seems you'll live to see another day, Mouse." His voice is cool, satisfied, and I realize that I've done that for him. I've given him pleasure. I'm so happy I almost smile. I proved myself to be useful even if it's just with my body. Maybe I should be ashamed of what I just did but oddly, I am not. Even more absurd is the fact that I enjoyed pleasuring Xander.

Before I can make a move and get up on my own, he leans down and picks me up like a child, just to deposit me onto the bed. I blink very slowly, trying to comprehend what is taking place. He removes his button-up shirt and tosses it to the floor.

I grip onto the sheets when he slides into the bed beside me. He's naked, and I have no panties on. The fact that I just gave him a blow job means nothing when I all but signed my virginity over to him. I tense slightly. I know it's going to happen so I might as well let him do it.

"Sleep. That's all we're doing tonight. You've proven yourself useful for now, but tomorrow you'll have to prove yourself again, and each day it will get harder and harder for me to see your worth to me. That is unless you're exceptional at fucking."

My chest constricts at his words, and when he tucks me into his side, I shiver. He pulls the rumpled comforter up and over us, and I feel the warmth of his body seep into every single bone in my body. For a moment, I think he must be playing a cruel joke on me. Letting me sleep in his bed with him, cuddling and keeping me warm and comfortable. It almost seems too good to be true, but he makes no move to make me think otherwise.

"Goodnight," he whispers into the hollow of my neck. And for a moment, I think I must have heard him wrong. My eyes start to drift closed very slowly, and even though I know I shouldn't... I feel safe, completely safe in this monster of a man's arms.

He said he was going to hurt me, but then he didn't. He said he was just like his dad, but he is nothing like him at all. He's killed for me, guided me instead of taking from me, and if that's not worthy of feeling safe then I'm not sure what is. Xander might think he's a monster, but I just can't see that that's all he is.

I close my eyes and drift off immediately, cuddled up in this comfortable bed.

I don't know how long I'm asleep but when I wake, I'm uncomfortably hot. Xander's arm is still slung over me and the heavy comforter on top hardly lets any body heat escape. My throat is painfully dry. I just need to get some water.

I wiggle myself out of the bed, trying not to wake him up. It's completely dark in the room now and I have to find my way to the bathroom by patting softly around. Sleep still makes my limbs heavy, and I can feel myself sway while walking.

When I finally get to the bathroom, I close the door very quietly behind me and flip on the light switch. The brightness instantly blinding me, I squeeze my eyes shut until they adjust.

I walk to the sink and dare to look in the mirror. Just like I expected, I look terrible. My cheek is an ugly blueish purple, my hair is an uncombed mess, my eyes are bloodshot, and my stupid wrists are painfully swollen now.

I turn on the cold water and splash some in my face before getting a drink straight from the faucet.

Why am I so hot?

Even the cold water didn't cool me down. I'm still really... *really* hot. My whole body, even my eyeballs feel hot. Shaking my head, I turn off the water and turn back to the door when something occurs to me... I'm not tied up or locked in. I don't think Xander's locked the room behind us.

I stand like a statue in the bathroom, a million thoughts running through my mind. Should I try to get away? Should I believe Xander's words and be scared for my life or should I trust my gut about him? This might be the only chance I get to get away... and all I can think about is my sister possibly dying at the hands of more vile men.

I have to run.

I should run.

6

Xander

I WAKE up in my bed like most mornings. Still, I know right away that something is off. I open my eyes to find it's already light outside. Rays of sunshine coming through the window make small specks of dust dance in the air.

I suck in a deep breath and catch the lingering sweet scent of a woman.

Shit!

I jump out of my bed, scanning the empty room. Where the fuck did she go? I pull on my pants and run out to the hallway. I'm so fucking angry right now I want to punch through the wall. I march down to the front door, ready to kill something. My guards are standing post exactly where they're supposed to be.

"Did anyone see the girl trying to leave?" I growl at them.

"No, boss, no one tried to leave."

"You two have been here all night?" I question angrily. How could I have been so dumb to think she wouldn't try and escape?

At their nods, my anger reaches new heights. "Search the house... every fucking inch and if I find out you let her get away, I'll kill you myself."

They both spring into action, headed in different directions, while I run back upstairs annoyed as fuck. Where the hell is she? I make it back to the room and look around again. Did she take anything? I don't think she did. Even my gun is in the drawer of my bedside table. Wouldn't that be the first thing you take? Maybe her intention wasn't to harm me? Maybe she just wanted to leave? Hell, there is no maybe about it. She wanted to leave. She begged to leave. I pull on a pair of jeans and a shirt, taking my gun and my phone.

I'm about the head back downstairs when my eyes move to the bathroom door. I realize then that in my haste to check the entire house, I hadn't even checked the bathroom. A possessive need to find her pushes me forward, and I grip the door handle.

I don't hear any noise coming from inside, but I open the door anyway. It's dark and quiet, and I almost turn around and slam the door shut when I see it... see her. Her tiny little body is huddled on the floor beside the toilet.

I flip on the light and rush inside. She is lying motionless on the floor. Her strawberry-blond hair fans out like a halo around her head, making her look like an angel.

Her eyes are closed, and her lips are slightly parted. At first glance, it seems like she is sleeping peaceful but when I kneel down beside her, I can hear her wheezing... struggling to breathe. I pick her up and realize how hot she is... not just hot... she is burning up. Her skin is on fire, and I know I have to do something.

Carrying her almost lifeless body to the tub, I place her inside gently before turning the water on cold. She's not going to like this, not even a little bit, but I don't care. I can't have my mouse dying. The ice-cold water hits her heated skin and she doesn't even flinch. Hell, she doesn't even move really and that tells me all I need to know.

Pulling out the phone from my back pocket, I scroll down until I find Doc Brown's number then I hit the green call button. Time seems to stand still as the phone rings and rings. My patience is running thin when he finally answers on the third ring.

"Hello?"

"I need you at my house asap."

"On my way, boss." That's why I like him. I call, and he comes running, no questions asked.

While we wait, I crouch down beside the tub, holding my little mouse's head above the cold water. For a moment, I wonder what the fuck I'm doing here. Why am I trying to save her life? This would be the easiest way out for both of us. She dies, and I don't have to pull the trigger myself.

She has to die anyway; why not let her go now? It would save her a lot of misery and free me from this weird hold she has over me. My fingers clutch her delicate skin... my gaze moving over face.

"Don't leave me, Mouse," I say out loud, shocked that I let them cross my lips.

Why does the thought of her dying feel like a fucking knife in my heart?

I sit in complete silence, listening to the water fill the tub. After a while, she seems to have cooled down enough and I turn off the water, letting it drain.

My white t-shirt clings wetly to her skin, letting me see every little curve underneath. Fuck... she is not wearing anything underneath. I try and avert my eyes, but I'm not a good man. Even in the state she's in, I still want to touch her.

Heavy footsteps meet my ears, and I know it's the doc finally getting here. The gray-haired man walks into the bathroom, looking down at the small body in the large bathtub. He takes in the situation, and without asking any questions, he kneels next to the tub and starts to examine her.

I hold back a growl as his hands move over her all but naked body. Watching him touch her infuriates me.

"It looks like the cuts on her wrists got infected." Fuck. Why didn't I bandage and dress the wounds last night?

"The infection has already spread up her arms and because she has two injuries, it's rapidly spreading. Her body can't keep up the fight against it. We need to get her on an IV and on antibiotics right away if she has a chance at making it. Do you know when she's last eaten or had something to drink?"

I shake my head and grind my teeth. My blood boils... I'm so fucking angry, and I have no one to blame but myself. I didn't even give her anything to eat or drink last night.

"Can you get the shirt off and move her to the bed? I'll get everything ready in there." He gets up and pauses for a second, a flicker of anxiety appearing in his eyes. "Unless you want to move her somewhere else. She might be out for a while."

"Here is fine."

I watch him leave the bathroom before I turn back to my little mouse... I don't even know her real name. I bet she has a beautiful name that fits her beautiful face. Shaking my head, I grip the collar of the shirt and start ripping it down the middle.

My dick twitches in my pants when I see her perfect little body underneath the shirt. Creamy smooth skin without a single blemish on her. A perfect pair of perky tits and a flat stomach.... a little too flat for my liking right now. I don't dare let my eyes wander all the way between her legs. A raging hard-on is the last thing I need right now.

I grab a towel from the rack and cover her up with it before I pick her up and carry her back to the bedroom. I look down at her in my arms; her eyes remain closed, her face peaceful with some strands of wet hair sticking to her forehead and cheek.

Her face is expressionless, and I realize then how much I miss the flicker of fear or even fire in her gaze. I place her on the bed where Doc. Brown is already setting up an IV.

"I'm gonna get her hooked up and then I'm going to have to re-open the wounds to let the infection drain out. After that, I'll wrap them up."

I watch the doctor work on her for a few minutes before I can't stand watching him touch her any longer. I know he is helping her but that doesn't mean I don't want to slap his hand away every time he touches her skin.

Stepping out of the room, I try to get all these irrational feelings under control. I need a fucking reality check. Walking down to the end of the hall, I end up in front of my son's nursery.

I open the door quietly, just in case he is sleeping, but as soon as I pop my head inside the door, I discover he is not.

One of the nannies is holding him in her arms, feeding him a bottle. His tiny fingers are trying to grab the bottle and his little lips are sucking on the nipple like he hasn't eaten in years... just as he always does.

"Do you want to feed him today?" Maria asks. She is his caregiver most of the time and Q loves her.

"No, I just wanted to see him really quick." Seeing him always quiets the storm inside me momentarily.

This is all that matters... him. Suddenly, a crazy idea enters my mind, an image that I can't shake now that it's in my head. I imagine my little mouse sitting in here with my son... feeding him. I think he would like her. She would love him. I don't know how I know... I just do.

No, I can't think of something like this. I could never trust her with my son; I don't even know her. I threatened to hurt and kill her. I could never trust her with him. For all I know, she is just a really fucking good actress and is spying on me for my father.

I can't let my guard down. Not with her or anybody else. My family counts on me.

When I get back to my bedroom, the doc is just wrapping up her wrists.

He looks up when he hears me coming in. "You need to keep her arms elevated. I'll come and check on her again in the morning. Until then, watch the red marks on her arms. If they spread, call me back right away. Here are some pain meds and some antibiotics."

He sits two pill bottles down on my nightstand before examining me nervously. "Is that all I can get for her? Or does she need anything else... like the morning after pill?"

His question infuriates me beyond all reasoning. I know logically it shouldn't.

She is, after all, a beautiful young girl half naked in my bathroom, and she clearly has been tied up. Of course, he would assume she'd been raped, as it wouldn't be the first time I've done something psychologically fucked. I know his assumption shouldn't bother me... but fuck, it does.

"Don't ask questions, Doc. If I needed something else, I'd have asked. Now, if you're needed, I'll call you. Otherwise, get the fuck out." I grit out the words and he scurries from the bedroom, grabbing his things.

As soon as we're alone, I settle onto the side of the bed and stare at her. I watch her chest rise and fall beneath the blanket... I listen to the medicine drip from the IV bag into the tube and watch the saline being carried through it to the needle in her arm. This, her being here, me saving her, it's so unlike me.

I'm a killer, not a savior, and still, I cannot shake the hold this tiny girl has over me.

"Who are you?" I whisper, trailing a knuckle down the side of her cheek. Her skin is still hot, but a sheen of sweat coats her forehead, telling me her fever is breaking.

I think of the things she told me yesterday... of how she merely went searching for her sister. She was selfless walking into a den full of lions. I'm surprised I didn't find her in worse condition. Then again, my father hadn't really gotten a chance to touch her. If he had, I can guarantee she'd wish she was dead.

Isn't that what you'll do to her? Make her wish she was dead by the time you're done with her? I squeeze my eyes shut. I don't understand the feelings coursing through me. The only thing that is clear is that I cannot hurt her. I can't... no matter what.

"Xander..." My name falls from her lips on a whimper and I look up, expecting her to be awake, but she's not. I grab onto her fragile hand that's extended outward on the bed. I interlace our fingers... She's useless to me like this, our agreement null and void.

On top of it, she's a loose end. If anyone discovers her, then everything will unravel. I stop myself from thinking further on the matter. I'm not in the right state of mind right now.

My need for her is causing me to break every fucking rule that I put into place, and secretly, my father is getting his way. He may not know it, but I do. He's left me something, someone, that I cannot bring myself to kill.

And it's going to ruin everything...

It already has.

7

Ella

MY EYES BURN, my head throbs, and a coldness fills my veins. I try and swallow, but my throat burns feels like fifty-grit sandpaper. My tongue is heavy in my mouth and every single breath I take is labored. I try and lift my arms and legs but nothing works. I feel broken. I will my eyes to open, but they don't.

"Her fever is back up." A deep rumbling voice fills my ears.

"That's going to happen, boss. She's fighting an infection. It'll be a couple of days before we see any real improvement." That same voice lets out a loud sigh, and I feel the bed dip beside me. I flicker through the memories in my mind... trying to put a face to the voice.

The image of a man with dark hair and even darker eyes appears before me.

Xander.

"Don't die on me, Mouse," he whispers, so softly I barely hear him. I think I feel his lips graze my forehead, but I cannot be sure. Questions burn deep inside of me. Why is he caring for me? Shouldn't he have just killed me? I'm not of any use to him now.

Our agreement appears in my mind, and I wonder if he's going to end things now. He probably should. It would be easier, right? I feel trapped, caught between four walls that are slowly closing in around me. I cannot cry or scream. I can't do anything to let him know that I am here... with him. I try and mumble, move my limbs, anything at all, but everything starts to fade out again. A buzzing fills my ears and within seconds, I'm gone... floating through endless darkness. Maybe I'm already dead? I can't tell the difference between reality and dream anymore.

When I awake again, it feels like it's only been a second, but there is no way that is possible. Warmth blankets my body, and I want to snuggle deep into it. I wonder why I'm unable to move or speak but can't communicate my fears.

After what seems like an eternity, I am finally able to peel my eyes open again. I blink a few times, making sure I'm really awake now and not still in limbo. My surroundings become clearer with each blink and then I suddenly see the person sitting in front of me.

"Welcome back to life, little mouse."

For a long time, I just look at him. I'm still trying to put all the pieces back together.

How did we end up in this moment? I feel like I am missing part of the story. Unable to connect from offering him my body for survival to him caring for me in his bed. Something must have happened in between those two events that I don't know about.

"Why?" It hurts to speak but I ask the question anyway.

Xander's brow furrows in confusion as if he doesn't understand what I am saying. "What do you mean why?"

I try and say something else, but I cannot get the words past my lips. Xander passes me a glass with water in it, and I take it into my shaky hands. As soon as it touches my dry lips, I swallow it down, drinking from the cup greedily until Xander pries it from my grasp.

"That's enough. You'll get sick if you drink too much, too fast."

I nod in understanding, placing my hands in my lap. I realize then as the soft sheets move against my bare skin that I am, in fact, completely naked.

Did we? Did he? My mind is a mess of thoughts, but I'm certain I'd remember if we had done anything to that extent. I lift my gaze to his. He's watching me again, his face void of emotion, and I wonder why he does that. Hides his emotions from the people he's talking to. Maybe he thinks he's safe that way? I don't really know, but when it comes to understanding others, I always try and read between the lines, and reading between the lines is the only way I think Xander can be understood.

"Why did you care for me?" I finally ask.

Xander smirks. "There is no way I was going to let you die before I got to claim your virgin pussy, Mouse. Good pussy is hard to come by now a days."

My cheeks heat immediately. He cannot actually mean that, right? He didn't save me just so he could fuck me.

"I don't believe you," I blurt out, feeling hurt. I remember his lips on my forehead, his voice a beacon of light in the darkness.

Xander smiles, and it's sinister, sickening, and suddenly I wish I never asked him why he saved me. "How do you know I didn't already fuck you?"

"Because you're not that vile of a monster." I regret the words as soon as they're spoken. In a second, Xander is above me, his hand wrapped around my throat. Fear spikes deep inside of me. Had I just fought an infection only to die because I can't keep my mouth shut?

Xander leans into my face. I can smell him; his scent surrounds me. His mouth is inches from mine, and I consider what may happen if I were to kiss him, but the thought slips away as soon as he starts to speak.

"I'm every bit as vile as my father, and I'll do to you the same fucking things he will. Don't think that just because I saved your life that I want you around for more than a hole to fuck. You're nothing, Mouse, nothing but a place for my dick."

I feel my lips trembling, and tears blur my vision. "Okay," I whisper softly, all while knowing deep down inside he has no idea that I heard his words, that I know how he truly feels. That his voice brought me out of the darkness and back to harsh reality.

In an instant, he's off of me and pushing from the bed.

"Our agreement is still on. I'll give you twenty-four more hours to gain your strength but that's all the mercy you'll receive from me."

I don't understand the hot and cold he gives off. I know he wanted me to live. I heard the anguish in his words, but now that I am awake, he seems angry, as if he had hoped that I wouldn't make it.

"You could've just left me to die. You didn't have to put all this work into it," I whisper, pushing up on the mattress, trying to right myself into a more seated position while pulling the blanket up and over chest. I feel something pulling at my arm and look down to see what looks like a spot for an IV that must've been put into my arm.

"And let you die so easily?" I lift my gaze to his and find amusement twinkles in his eyes. "I think it'd be funner to fuck you until you can't take anymore, then let you just fade away from illness."

His words are cruel, so very cruel, but I can't lash out at him for saying them. No, that'll just get me killed, and I'm already running on borrowed time. Yet I let my next words escape my lips without thought.

"You don't mean that, Xander."

"And why the fuck not?" He stops dead in his tracks, looking every bit the monster that he wants everyone to believe he is.

"Because I heard you. I heard you tell me not to die. I know you didn't want to lose me."

He clenches his fists at his sides and then strides right back over to the bed. I wonder for a second if he will actually hurt me. The fire in his eyes flickers, and I know I've gone and fanned the damn flames, igniting an inferno deep inside of him.

Gripping the edge of the blanket, he pulls it from my grasp. I gasp at the sudden coldness that blankets my skin, stealing every ounce of warmth from my body.

I feel his gaze on my bare body and try and cover myself up with my hands. I swallow around the knot of fear that I cannot get to go down. When I feel his hands grip onto my thighs and pry them apart with brute strength, I cry out. Why can't I just keep my mouth shut?

"Please, no…" I don't want this to happen this way, not between us. I thrash back and forth against the mattress, feeling my already weakened body giving out.

"But isn't that what you want? Me to show you how big and bad I can truly be? Don't you want to see how far I'll go before I snap?" he snarls directly into my face. His fingers break my thighs apart and I feel him, his hand hot at my center.

Without further warning, he slams two fingers inside me and holds them there. My body stiffens at the sudden intrusion, but when he doesn't move, I can feel myself soften into his touch. His eyes roam over bare body, the heat in them slowly dissipating.

By the time he reaches my face, his eyes have completely softened, and it seems as if he's lost the sharp jagged edge needed to push forward.

The fear I felt moments before fizzles away into warmth that fills my belly. Feeling his thick fingers inside me makes me long with need. I feel full, impossibly full, but it doesn't hurt. A long silence stretches between us but neither one of us breaks eye contact.

Then he starts moving out of me slowly and before I know what I'm doing, I grab his wrist, holding him in place.

Confusion flickers across his eyes briefly. "Do you want me to make you come, Mouse?" His voice is kind, soft, and I already know the answer.

I bite my bottom lip nervously. "Yes," I murmur almost inaudibly.

An evil grin tugs on his lips, and he starts moving his finger back inside of me. My breath hitches. Now that my body was expecting it, my reaction to his touch changes.

His fingers inside me don't feel like an intrusion any longer. They feel like they belong there and nowhere else. He moves them in and out of me in a slow steady rhythm and it feels like heaven. I have to fight the urge to close my eyes in pleasure because for some strange reason, I want to see him looking at me, watching me as I fall apart.

My hold on his wrist is firm, but only because I want to touch him, and I'm not sure where else he'll allow me to put my hands.

Pleasure zings through me with every deep stroke of his fingers. My heart flutters around inside my chest like a butterfly trying to break free. His movements are gentle, kind, and it's so unlike him, unlike the man he wants me to believe he is that it's almost terrifying.

"Come for me, Mouse. Come all over my hand." He stares me down, pulling the pleasure out of me with nothing more than a command.

A small moan I can't hold back escapes me. My chest heaves, feeling things I've never felt before. My nipples pucker, and my body shivers. My pussy clenches, squeezing his fingers hard, but he continues his slow and sensual strokes and then he curls his fingers upward inside me, hitting some spot that draws unbelievable pleasure out of me.

Unable to keep my eyes open any longer, they shut without me wanting them to. My head falls back into the pillow as a wave of pleasure washes over me, taking with it pieces of my soul. My body tingles and I lie there for a moment, trying to get my eyes to open again. When I do, he removes his fingers just as quickly as he entered them.

I feel cold at the loss of his touch, and I reach for the blanket, wrapping it around my body. I don't even get a chance to say anything to him because he's up and out the door in a flash, leaving me behind in his bed, breathless and more confused than ever.

What the hell just happened?

Again, he's hot, hotter than the sun and then cold in an instant, as if something inside him snaps and he turns off that viciousness.

He wants to be kind to me. I can feel it and see it, even if he doesn't want me to. He is kind, and that's the part of him I think he's scared of most... me seeing him as more than the monster hidden in the shadows.

8

Xander

I HAD to walk out of that room before I did something I would regret. What I wanted to do to her would have hurt her... I wanted to strip myself bare and fuck her senseless. I'd never been one to hold myself back from something I wanted, but my timid little mouse is bringing out the good in me.

I'd planned on fingering her roughly to show her exactly who it was she was dealing with, and yet again, I somehow managed to tamp down the darkness rushing through my veins. She fell apart on my hand, and I swear it was the sexiest goddamn thing I've ever had the pleasure of witnessing.

Bringing the fingers that were inside her channel not so long ago to my lips, I lick them clean, sucking on them, still tasting her release on them. My cock hardens painfully, and I stop mid-step. I could turn around and make her suck me off... I clench my jaw, still feeling slightly on edge. The thought is very tempting, but I think it's best to leave things the way they are right now, even more so since I called a meeting this morning.

I walk downstairs and into my office. My gaze lands on Damon, who's already waiting for me. He's early, earlier than usual, and he's sitting in front of my desk, his feet propped up on it, looking as if I had left him waiting for hours. I don't like the look he's giving me, not even a fucking little.

"You can wipe that annoying look off your face before I lose it and wipe it off for you... with my fist."

"Well, aren't we in a great mood today." Damon drops his feet from the desk, his gaze piercing mine. He has no idea... not even the slightest clue.

"Any update on Daddy Dearest?" Damon asks as I settle into the chair behind my desk.

All of this stuff with Mouse has had my head in the clouds. I haven't been able to focus on anything but her for the last couple of days, but now that she's awake, I feel like I can finally walk away from her without fear of her dying.

"Yes and no. Remember how I had asked you to keep your ear to the ground about her sister?"

Damon nodded.

"Well, she mentioned something about a flesh auction." I smirk. "And you remember how much Father loves those. I'll bet you anything that he is going to put some girls up. Maybe we can track him that way. Find the sister, see what she knows. Maybe she can lead us to him? It's a long shot but it's all we have right now."

"And once you find him, what are you going to do? Go in there guns blazing again?"

"What else are we going to do? The man has been hiding for years without us knowing."

The truth was my father had been hiding for a long time in the shadows. One of our guards helped him get away... I was so stupid not to make sure he was dead before having them haul his body away.

Betrayal didn't sit well with me, and I knew the moment I found out my father was alive someone had helped him. I remembered the guard and went to interrogate him. The look on his face when I confronted him was a mixture of fear and shock.

I'm sure he expected to die for his indiscretions, and he did.

"From the looks of it, he's been moving, never staying anywhere for too long."

I tap my long fingers against the desk. "That's because he knows we're coming for him. If he's smart, he'll keep moving, keep hiding, because when we get our hands on him, he'll be praying for a quick death. I'm hoping that I can find him at this auction and put an end to his disgraceful life."

Damon's expression mirrors my own. He wants to make certain our father dies, too. After all, he has a beautiful wife that he needs to protect.

"How is the girl?" He smirks, as if he knows the hell I've been through the last couple of days. I can't share with him the kindness I have shown her. Not because I don't want my brother to know I care about someone; he already knows I care about Q. I'd kill for him, but I didn't care for anyone who wasn't blood, and Mouse definitely wasn't blood.

"Fine," I answer, wiping my face of any emotion.

"Is she really fine?" he presses. "Because you look tired as hell, and I'm guessing it's not from being up all night with Q."

"I'm fine. She is fine. I haven't killed her yet, so I suppose that's good news, right?" I lift a brow.

Laughter bursts out of Damon's throat at my response. "I guess, but you can't really fuck a dead body...." He pauses, his gaze widening. "I mean, unless you're into that thing, and if so, you're fucking disgusting."

I shake my head at his nonsense. "Explain to me why I invited you here again?"

Truthfully, and I'd never tell my brother this, but I'd love having him back in the house. This place is as much his as it is mine and having him here with me reminds me of the power we'd hold over everyone if we'd work together.

"Honestly, I don't know, but I'm starting to think it's to annoy me." He pauses briefly, and I can tell he wants to say something. He rubs his hands down the front of his pants like he is nervous.

"Something you want to tell me?"

Damon's face deadpans, "Not really but since you shared Q with me, I guess I should share mine with you, so... Keira is pregnant."

I blink, then I force a smile. Men like my brother and I aren't cut out for the family life. The white picket fence and two and a half kids.

Looking at my brother's face, all I see is worry. "We need to get rid of him soon. I need to protect Keira and the baby just like you need to protect your son. He can't be alive much longer. We will never be safe as long as he is alive. If you're going to this auction, I want to go with you."

"I understand your worries, brother, but I need to think my choices through. I do want to go in guns blazing, but I know he'll be expecting that, and that's the last thing I want to give him. I need the element of surprise on our side. Plus, if you're so worried about Keira's safety then maybe you should stay here for a while."

He shakes his head. "You'd like that, wouldn't you? Having me at your beck and call."

I roll my eyes. He's starting to give me an attitude and, brother or not, I wouldn't deal with that shit. "No, Damon. I wouldn't like that. I would fucking love it. We would be a force to reckon with if we came together as one."

Damon scrubs a hand down his face in frustration. "That's the difference between. You'll always be a heartless killer, while I've found a way to let love in. I can't kill and bathe in the blood of my enemies knowing that I have to go home and see my child's innocent face."

I clench my jaw hard. Every time it seemed like we were taking a step forward, Damon pulled us backward.

Shoving from my chair, I walk to the door to leave, my brother's eyes on me with every step. "I guess we don't have anything else to talk about then. We'll head out for Vegas in two days' time. For now, you're dismissed and should go home to your wife."

I gritted my teeth. This is what I wanted, right? Damon to have a good life? This was why I took all the beatings, why I became the heartless piece of shit that I am.

"Keira isn't home, she came with me. She didn't tell me, but I know she just wanted to come so she could see Q."

My head snaps back in the direction of Damon, my mind immediately drifting to the other person in a room not so far down that hallway.

I've told the nannies to not make a sound in the hallway and keep Q's door closed so Mouse wouldn't hear but Keira doesn't know about that.

I exhale slowly, trying to cool my heated blood. I really hope my mouse isn't dumb enough to leave my bedroom, even if she hears someone in the hallway. Unfortunately, I have a feeling she's doing just that... investigating. I scurry from the room without an explanation. He's a guest in my house so I don't really need to tell him where I'm hiding Mouse or what I'm doing with her.

"What the fuck? Did you forget a pie in the oven or something? Where are you going?" Damon calls out at my departure.

Dumbass.

I run up the stairs, every step I take confirming the feeling that I'm right... *Please, Mouse... please.* She's a smart girl. She wouldn't test my kindness or what very little of it that I have, would she?

I try to keep a level head. *Remember, you don't want to hurt her.* But I know I'll do whatever I need to do to protect my son.

As soon as I turn the corner at the top of the stairs and look down the hallway, I see my nightmare coming to life. I lose control, my heart vibrates through me, fear for the safety of my son consumes me.

It's just two women standing in the middle of the hallway, talking like they are old friends meeting for some coffee but to me, it's a sign of betrayal... from both of them each in their own way.

"Hey..." Keira notices me first and her eyes go wide at my appearance. Whatever she was going to say is cut off in her throat.

Looking at them, all I can fucking think about is that I need to protect my son.

She knows... she knows about him. I feel like I've somehow failed my little boy. Bringing her here was a mistake. Keeping her alive an even worse idea.

I clench my fists, my muscles tightening with anger. There is no going back now. There is only one way out for her now, and it's not alive.

My legs start moving on their own, heading straight for my mouse... my enemy... I see red. I need to take her out, protect my family. Her big blue doe eyes go impossibly wide, and even from a few feet away I can see that she is shaking.

The smell of her fear tickles my nose and hardens my cock.

"Take Q to his room, Keira!" I order without looking at her. "Now!"

I cross the distance between us before anyone else makes a move. Mouse tries to take a step away from me but I'm much too fast. I take her upper arm into my hand and yank her toward me, making her wince.

"Why didn't you stay in the fucking room?" I mutter more as a question to myself than to her. She doesn't answer, and maybe she doesn't have an answer, or maybe she thought she was safe, I don't know. But instead of talking, she just starts crying, most likely hoping that her tears will have an effect on me... and they do, they crack me wide open. But I can't show her mercy, not on this, not when it comes to protecting my son.

My fingers dig into her soft flesh, and I know when I release her, she'll have bruises. She starts struggling, trying to get away from me but my grip on her is unyielding.

Fight all you want, Mouse... all it does is make me want you more.

Out of the corner of my eyes, I see Keira finally moving. "You're hurting her. Let her go!"

"Shut the fuck up and mind your own business," I sneer.

"Hey, don't talk to her like that." Damon appears from the staircase, his face a mask of horror as if he cannot believe that I'd fucking talked to his wife so harshly. My head is spinning, emotions I don't understand firing off inside of it.

"Get your wife on a fucking leash then." I start dragging Mouse by her arm in the direction of the staircase but she digs her heels into the marble floor. I almost laugh at the pitiful excuse of a human she is. She's weak, tiny, and she thinks that she can fight me, that she can escape my grasp?

"Please, Xander," she begs with a shaky voice, panic written clearly on her doll-like features. Her soft pleas for me to stop are fucking with my head. Aggravated, I bend down to pick her up, throwing her over my shoulder. Her belly lands hard against my shoulder, and I hear the distinct swoosh of air leaving her lungs.

"You should have stayed in the room," I growl and walk past Damon. His eyes meet mine briefly and I know he's silently judging me, most likely hoping I'll let her go but he has no idea what I have planned for my tiny mouse, not a fucking clue. I descend the stairs, Mouse's tiny fists beating against my back.

"Damon, do something!" Keira yells in the quickly fading background.

"Stay out of it, baby." At least my brother hasn't completely lost his mind.

I quickly make my way down to the basement, all with Mouse crying hysterically on my shoulder, her tiny hands fisting into my shirt. I can feel the heat of her body through my t-shirt and half of me wants to put her down and fuck her against the wall, showing her who owns her body, and soul. But I don't... even as my cock strains against my pants.

You brought this on yourself, Mouse.

Walking into the cell, I try to put her down onto the cot, but she is clinging to me, throwing her slender arms around my neck, pulling me closer.

"Please, Xander... Please, don't leave me down here."

"Shut up." I don't want to listen to her begging. I don't want to hear the longing in her voice. I want to erase it all from my memory. I want to go back in time and be strong enough to pull the fucking trigger. I pull her off of me, peeling her limbs from my body while she desperately tries to hold onto me like I'm her life jacket and she's seconds away from slipping into the dark deep ocean water.

When I finally peel her fingers from my back, I throw her small fragile body onto the cot and step out of the cell, closing the door behind me before she can even get up from the bed. I only catch her eyes for a second... hurt, panic, and betrayal reflect back at me.

I know she doesn't understand why I'm doing this.

Of course, she doesn't.

She will never understand why I do the things I do. And that is why this can never work. My sweet little mouse will only ever be an example of everything I can never have.

"I'm sorry... Xander, I'm sorry for leaving the room. I should have stayed in there. I'm sorry. I just heard someone and..."

My fingers make their way into my hair, and I tug on the long strands. Her pleas are maddening. "Stop! Just... stop... I don't want to hurt you... I really fucking don't, but if you don't shut up, if you don't stop... I will, Mouse. I'll hurt you." My voice is strained and when I hear the soft whimpers escape her lips, I turn on my heels and walk back up the steps and away from her. When I reach the top floor, I hope and pray that the noise inside my head calms soon.

9

Ella

I watch him disappear from my view and listen to his heavy footsteps fade away into the distance. I curl into a ball on the cold cot, wishing I was anywhere but here. Had I not been stupid enough to go searching for my sister, I wouldn't be here right now.

My chest constricted with every breath I take. I don't know what I did wrong but seeing Xander so angry with me hurt. It hurt like hell.

Why didn't I just stay in the damn room? I know why... I was just so curious hearing a female voice right outside the door. I hadn't had any interaction with anyone besides Xander, and his guards, who didn't even look at me. So, hearing an unfamiliar voice, a female one at that, made me want to investigate... All I wanted was to talk to someone.

I bite my bottom lip to stop it from trembling.

How could I have known that I'd find that woman holding a baby? And that the baby was Xander's son... Tears slip from my eyes and down my cheeks. Xander, the man cloaked in darkness, has a son, an innocent little boy.

The image of the way he looked at me when he saw me standing next to that woman... I can't get it out of my mind. He looked feral, like a momma bear rescuing her cubs.

Still, the question lingered in the air. Why did he get so mad at me? Did he think I would harm his son? I had a lot of questions and no answers, and once again, I was in the cold, dark, basement. I forced myself to stop crying... swallowing down the fear that pumped through my veins.

He didn't want to hurt me. I felt it in his touch and heard it in the pitch of his voice. I'm safe here and after our agreement is done, after I'd given myself to him, I'll walk away free. I tell myself this over and over again, because if I don't, I'm going to break down into a sobbing mess. Xander hadn't promised me anything, but I felt deep down in my heart that he will let me go.

He's an evil man, but I'm starting to realize I am his kryptonite. Snuggling deeper into myself, I close my eyes, trying to force myself to go to sleep, since that seems to be the only way out of here at the moment.

I only doze off for a few minutes before the sound of approaching footsteps has me sitting straight up on the cot, my eyes open and my body on high alert.

Who is coming? Is it another one of his men? The thought makes me feel dirty.

My heart rate picks up with every step I hear echo throughout the basement until finally Xander comes into view. I take a relaxing breath the moment I see him, but that relaxation is short lived. He is still angry. I can see it in his eyes, though the fury from earlier has simmered. He's still mad, and that's something to watch out for.

I trust Xander, even though I shouldn't. After all, he's given me no real reason not to.

I watch eagerly as he pulls out a set of keys and unlocks the cell. I want to jump up and fall into his arms, but I don't want to be too hasty. He might not even be here to get me. So, instead, I just wait motionless on the edge of the bed, waiting for him to say something.

When he doesn't, a nervous knot starts to form in my belly. Is he going to leave me down here all night? I want to plead with him, start begging him, but I remember his words, his desire to hurt me if I didn't shut up. Shock fills me when he strolls across the floor and bends down to pick me up, sliding one arm under my legs and the other under my shoulders.

I put my arms around him and bury my face into the crook of his neck, taking in a deep breath, letting his unique scent fill my nose. My freezing skin on his warm body drives all my coldness away and replaces it with warmth.

"I know you want me to believe you're a horrible man, but I don't. I feel safe with you," I whisper into his skin, near his ear.

He stiffens but continues walking. "You're the only person I know that would say that they feel safe in my presence." His voice booms loudly in my ears.

"I do." I swallow. "I know I shouldn't. I know this is fucked up on so many levels, but I do, and I want you to know that…" I gaze down at his shirt-clad chest. "I didn't mean to scare you with your... son."

Xander's grip on my body tightens just as we reach the bedroom, and he deposits me onto the mattress. Then he walks over to the dresser and grabs something before going into the bathroom with a cup. I hear the faucet turn on and assume he's getting a glass of water. When he appears before me a few seconds later with his hand extended outward with the glass of water and a little white pill, I take them from him.

He watches me intently as I take them. I shiver at his eyes upon my skin, they mark every inch of my skin with heat.

"My son means the most to me, and you discovering him has ruined our perfectly integrated plans."

My eyes widen at his words. "What do you mean? I thought we had an agreement?"

The dim lighting in the room makes it hard to gauge Xander's expression but when I see the evil smirk on his lips, I know something has changed. He walks over to the nightstand on the opposite side of the bed and pulls something out. When he walks back over to me, I catch a glimpse of the item in his hands.

Handcuffs? Is this it? Is he just going to take from me, before finally putting a bullet in my head? How could I be so stupid? Why did I leave the room? He had been so kind to me... kinder than his father ever would've been.

"I see your brain conjuring up all kinds of things." His voice sounds dangerous, and when I move back slowly onto the mattress, he's right there invading my space. He's huge, and intimidating and as I move, the shirt I'm wearing rides up my thighs.

My eyes move up his body, stopping once they reach his dark orbs, but he won't meet my eyes and that terrifies me more than I care to admit. "Last time someone tied me to the bed it wasn't all that fun."

"And I can't promise that this time is going to be fun either." He snatches my arm and slaps the cuff on me over my still-bandaged wrist, attaching it to the headboard. I know better than to fight. The metal will only dig into my wound, and maybe that's what he wants, me helpless, unable to fight him off. Then he takes the other cuff and tightens it on my other wrist.

Panic floods my body along with memories from the night I was at Xander's father's mercy. The things he said to me. The way he touched me. I suck in a ragged breath and squeeze my eyes shut, trying to forget that day completely.

"You know I can never let you leave now, right?"

My eyes fly back open. "What do you mean? What about the arrangement?"

"It's still on... partially at least. I can let you live, but I can't let you walk out of here, not with you knowing about my son. I won't be able to let you leave... ever."

I take a moment for his words to sink in. Am I supposed to stay the rest of my life in this room? How am I going to find my sister if I'm trapped here? There's no way I'll stay here. I'll escape or I'll die trying. I keep the thought to myself, burying it momentarily.

"So, you'll just keep me tied up in your bed like a sex slave?" I spit the words, anger filling my belly. Xander's hot and cold behavior confuses me. Every time I think I know what to expect from him, he surprises me.

"Until I get my fill of you, yes. Then I'll most likely pass you on to someone else. Probably one of my guards. It merely depends on how tight your pussy holds my cock."

Bile rises in my throat at his words. If there is any thought worse than being at Xander's mercy, it is being passed around like a slab of meat. I don't want anybody else touching me. This is not the deal we made. If I have to give myself to someone then I want it to be Xander.

"I want you, no one else." I make my desire for him apparent, spreading my legs slightly. I watch his gaze move over my bare legs and my spread thighs.

"I don't think you know what you're asking for right now, Mouse."

I visibly gulp, because he's right. I don't. But I also don't want to die, not before I get a chance to find my sister.

"I probably don't, but I don't want to die, and I don't want someone besides you to touch me. If I'm no use to you then I'm as good as dead and being dead isn't going to help me find my sister." I confess the words so quietly, as if they're a sin. "Just let me go eventually, please."

"You'll stay here however long I say... I might not have told you to stay in this room, but you should've known better. Instead, you took my kindness for something else. So, you'll remain mine until I say otherwise." His words sting, and I'm not sure why. It's not like they're not true.

"As for your sister, I have a small hunch on where she's going to be, and I'll be taking a trip in a few days to see if my hunch is correct."

I shoot into a sitting position, the cuff digging painfully into my wrist as I do so. I let out a low hiss, pushing the pain away.

"You know where she is?" Excitement bubbles to the surface. "You've been looking for her?"

Xander's face remains placid as he starts taking off his clothing, stripping down to nothing but a pair of boxers. My mouth waters and for a moment, I forget what we were talking about. His muscles look as if they've been carved from stone. I want to touch them.

Xander's voice breaks the hold his body has on my mind, pulling me back into the conversation. "I believe I know where she is, but you shouldn't get your hopes up. She could be dead. Women don't last long in this world, especially not the innocent type."

My heart aches at the thought of my sister being dead. We've lost everyone we ever loved, all we have left is each other. Losing her would be... I can't even fathom it. It occurs to me then... the auction. He's going to go to the auction... that's the only place he could be going, right? Unless the auction's past?

"She's not dead. She's strong and smart. If anyone can make it, it's her." I think back to how Xander's father said the same thing... how she'll wish for death in the end.

I pretend to act blissfully unaware, but I won't let him leave here without me. Wherever he is going, he is taking me with him. A chuckle escapes Xander's kissable lips as he crawls into bed on the other side, pulling me flush against his body. I can feel the heat of his skin through the thin fabric of my shirt.

"Those are the most fun parts to break," he whispers into my ear, sending a flurry of goosebumps across my skin.

"If it's the most fun then why haven't you broken me? Why haven't you just taken what you want? You've had the chance many times."

The thick black comforter is pulled up over us, encompassing our warmth beneath it. Xander doesn't respond right away and for a moment, I think he won't.

"Breaking you would be no fun to me, Mouse... because I don't want you broken. I don't want to take from you. I want to give to you..."

I squeeze my thighs together, remembering the pleasure he gave me.

"But make no mistake. If you betray my trust. If you share anything about my son with anyone outside of this home... I'll do more than break you... I'll make you wish I pulled that trigger on the first day we met."

"I won't..." I pause momentarily, feeling my heart beat out of my chest. "I wouldn't ever endanger the life of a child."

Xander wraps an arm around me, burrowing his face into my neck, "Good, because his mother tried that and, as you can see, she's no longer with us."

His words startle me. "You... killed her?" I don't even want to know the answer to that question. When his lips ghost against my skin, I nearly moan out in pleasure.

"Yes, and if I'm willing to kill my son's mother to protect him, there is no saying what I'll do to you."

"What did she do?" I don't even know why I'm asking. I don't really want to know why he killed her, but something inside me needs to know.

"She tried to use our son against me... it didn't help that she never should've gotten pregnant in the first place, but I found out before I killed her just how she managed to do so. She was no one to me, and I kept her alive for my son. I tried to do the right thing, and she used my kindness against me." Parts of me feel sorry for Xander, while other parts of me want to escape this room and run very far away.

"I'd never hurt your son," I murmur. Truthfully, I never would. He's nothing but a baby. He didn't ask to be born and my anger toward his father isn't his fault.

"You say that now, but you have yet to discover how dark I can get. You have yet discover just how powerful I am. What happens when I hurt you and you want to get even with me? What happens?"

"Nothing."

"Why nothing, Mouse?" I can hear the curiosity in his tone. My eyes start to feel heavy as I lay beside him. I'm protected, secure, and for at least right now, safe.

"Because you won't hurt me, Xander. We both know that. No matter how dark you are, you won't hurt me," I whisper, feeling myself slowly fade into the abyss.

Xander's hot breath fans against my cheek, his scent surrounds me, and I sink deeper into it, breathing him in heavily.

"You're right, I don't think I would hurt you either. Because it would break you and breaking you, Mouse, would be my biggest mistake." This time, his words are nothing more than a whisper in my ear, but they cling to me, and sink deep into my heart.

~

JUST LIKE THE first night I slept in his bed, I wake up with Xander curled around my body. The only thing that is different today is that my arm is stretched out across the headboard where the handcuff is keeping it in place.

I wonder if he is going to cuff me every night now. He wouldn't have to... not now that he is helping me find my sister. Lying awake like this has me asking myself a number of questions. Like where did Xander sleep when I was lying sick in his bed? Did he just lie down next to me or did he sleep somewhere else?

My thoughts dissolve into thin air when Xander stirs beside me, pulling me in closer to his chest. I feel his stiff erection press into my backside, and I wonder if I should be scared?

"I like waking up like this... with you at my complete disposal," he whispers into my ear, sleep coating his voice. His hand finds my hip and pulls my ass into his groin. My body stiffens in panic. Is this it? Am I about to lose my virginity?

"Don't worry, Mouse, I'll give you another day to heal. I want you to be good and well when I fuck you." He peels himself away from me and gets up from the bed. A moment later, he is back with the handcuff key. He unlocks them but leaves them hanging at the headboard. I rub at my wrists as soon as they're free.

"Go use the bathroom," he orders.

I do as he says and disappear into the bathroom. I do my business, wash my face, and brush my teeth with the new toothbrush Xander has laid out for me. Dread sinks deep into my belly. The thought of going back into the bedroom knowing that he is going to cuff me back to the bed makes me sick, but I can't hide in here forever.

So, with a sigh, I step out and find Xander waiting for me in the same spot I left him. I force my feet to move even though I don't want to. I get back on the bed and crawl over to him. I lift my gaze to his, praying but knowing he won't leave me uncuffed.

"You don't have to keep me cuffed to the bed. I won't leave the room," I say but give him my hand anyway.

He takes it without giving me a response, tightening the cuff around my wrist. "I have some work to do and I can't worry about you while I'm doing it. It's either the cuffs or the cell."

I just nod, the answer to his question is obvious. I don't want to go back into that basement... not after watching him kill that man. I sit back against the pillows and watch him get dressed. My mouth waters slightly. I know I shouldn't be attracted to him, but I can't help it. His body looks as if it is cut from stone, each muscle just as defined as the next.

"I'll bring you up some breakfast in a bit." He leaves the room. As soon as he is gone, the room feels empty and cold. I feel alone, but it's not the same kind of alone I've experienced in the last month. No, this kind of alone is different.

It's like I'm lost, unsafe, without him here, which is crazy, considering he's the one who's threatened to kill me numerous times. I can't wrap my head around the things I'm feeling. I pull the blanket around me with my free hand and curl up into myself, wondering if he is ever going to trust me again.

I spend the whole day in bed, which isn't terrible, considering I'm not feeling one hundred percent yet. Xander comes and goes throughout the day, bringing me meals and uncuffing me so I can go to the bathroom. I crave his company more than I realize. Every single time he leaves, I catch myself wishing he was here in bed with me. It's a strange feeling to have for someone you know could and most likely will harm you. But his company excites me. Every time I hear the creaking of the door or heavy footfalls, I get excited.

Then when he opens the door and I see him, I can't help but smile. He doesn't smile back at me, but I swear I can see it in his eyes... he is happy to see me, too. The hours seem to pass by as slow as molasses. I doze off here and there, awakening when he finally comes back to the room that night. I watch him take his clothes off in the dim lighting. He doesn't say anything to me right away and that's okay. It's not his words I really care to have, it's just his company. When he crawls under the blanket and pulls me into his side, I shiver.

"Tomorrow, Mouse... Tomorrow I will be inside of you. I can't wait any longer...and I won't. I need to make you mine."

"Okay, tomorrow." My belly tightens at the thought but only partially in fear. I don't want to think about tomorrow right now. "I wish you could have stayed in bed with me today."

There's a long pause, and I feel his nose burrow into my hair. He inhales my scent as if he needs it and that makes me safe, secure.

"Trust me, I would have liked that, too, but I had to make sure everything was is in order for us to leave tomorrow. I had to make sure my son is going to be protected when I'm gone. And then I needed to make sure we had enough men going tomorrow so that you would be protected."

A smile tugs at my lips. Once again, I am reminded that there is a man, a good man beneath the armored plate of murder and mayhem that is Xander.

There's a man who wants to be loved, a man who *can* be loved, if he allows it. Knowing that makes me want to do my best to reach that part of him because regardless of everything that's happened, he's trying his best to save me. He's trying his best to protect the people he loves from the darkness of his world.

And whether he thinks so or not, he's worth trying to save.

10

Xander

I WAKE UP SLOWLY, the warmth of Mouse's body beside mine. She is still sleeping, her body relaxed and molded perfectly into my embrace. My dick is rock hard, pressing up against her soft ass. I told her yesterday I would give her another day to heal...

Well, time's up, my little mouse. I slide my boxers down and kick them off under the blanket before I pull her back into my embrace.

With a grin, I slide my hand underneath the shirt she is wearing, my fingers gently stroking the perfectly smooth skin underneath it. Her skin is so soft, so untouched. I trail over her flat belly... all the way up to her perky little tits. I palm one, enjoying how well it fits in my hand.

She's the perfect fit, from the way her body reacts to mine, to the way she believes in me, like I'm some knight in shining armor.

A low moan fills the room and she pushes her ass into my hardness, probably not even realizing she is doing it. Still, knowing she reacts to my touch this way makes me smile. Plucking at her small nipple, I roll it gently between my thumb and pointer finger, drawing yet another moan out of her.

She sucks in a deep breath and lifts her head a little like she is looking around. I can't see her face like this, but I know she is awake now.

"Xander...?" Her voice is still thick with sleep, but I can sense the uncertainty in it. She has no idea what she is in for, but I can promise she'll enjoy every second of it.

"Your twenty-four hours are up," I whisper softly into her ear and feel her whole body stiffen at my words. All the sleep left her in an instant. The cuffs rattle as if she is tugging on them, making sure she still can't get away.

"There is nowhere to run to, Mouse," I whisper in her ear as my hand travels back down her body slowly. Her breath hitches when I arrive at my final destination. I dip my fingers between her legs and into her hot center. Finding her clit, I rub it gently with my palm while pressing one thick digit into her tightness.

"I didn't know it'd happen so soon." She rolls slightly, her big blue eyes piercing mine. I can see she's scared, smell it on her skin, but she doesn't have to be.

"I'm a lot of things, but a patient man, I am not." I sit up, spreading her legs real wide, my finger gently stroking her. Her chest starts to heave, and I love having her at my mercy.

I lick my lips and drop my gaze down to her tight cunt. My finger sinks inside her with ease, confirming her need for me. She's growing slicker with each stroke.

"I want to taste you. I want you to come on my tongue." I move slowly, dipping my head between her thighs. "Do you want that? To fall apart on my tongue while I finger you?" I look up at her over her mound. She's so fucking beautiful it hurts. Her strawberry-blonde hair is a mess, her big eyes looking down at me with desire and uncertainty.

Even though she's still afraid of me, she nods, most likely assuming I wouldn't stop if she asked me. But I would... I don't want to break my precious mouse.

I lower my face all the way to her skin so I can drag my tongue right across her clit, making her shudder. She tastes better than I could have ever imagined. Like the sweetest honey there is. I keep licking her, swirling my tongue around the little bundle of nerves while simultaneously sliding my finger in and out of her tight pussy. My cock is so hard it hurt.

Don't worry, buddy, soon... very soon.

Mouse moans and pants underneath me. Her body's getting restless, moving and pushing up into my face. Closing my lips around her clit, I suck on it lightly, making her body arch off the bed an inch. I know she is close and as much as I want to draw this out, my need to have my dick inside her is stronger.

So, with every last shred of patience inside me, I thrust my finger inside of her a few more times while I suck on her clit hard, flicking the bud back and forth, making her cry out my name and arch off the bed in earnest. Her already tight walls grip onto my finger, squeezing it tightly.

Fuck.

Her thighs quiver and the air expels from her lungs as she explodes around my finger. I ease my finger out of her and replace it with my tongue. My heart pounds furiously as I suck every drop of her release into my mouth. It'd been years since I went down on a woman, but Mouse deserved my tongue.

Shudders of pleasure run through her, and she tries to escape me, pulling her tiny hips back. But there is no escaping me, for as long as I am breathing, I will own Mouse. With one final lick between her folds, I pull away, easing up onto my knees.

Mouse's eyes widen as I move, grabbing a condom from the nightstand.

"Will you... will you be gentle?"

I grin down at her, the darkness blurring in my eyes. I don't want to be gentle. I want to lose control, but not yet... soon.

"As gentle as I can be..." I trail off, rolling the condom onto my length. I'm bigger than the typical male, and the idea of tearing her rips me apart. I want to have sex with her again as soon as fucking possible and that can't happen if she's hurt, so I have to take her with precision and a kindness that I know I don't fucking have.

She licks her lips nervously, and I grab a pillow, lifting her hips and placing it beneath her creamy white ass. As my eyes roam over her, I realize she is still cuffed to the bed, tugging against the restraints. I don't want her to hurt her wrists again, so I undo them, and her arms fall to the mattress with a thud. I pump my cock in my hand a few times, between her thighs, while my other hand grips onto her hip, holding her into place.

My entire body is on fire, need pumping through my veins. Probing her entrance with the head of my cock, I hear her gasp as I push into her slowly, so fucking slowly. I don't want to hurt her, but I fucking want that tightness, that sweet spot deep inside her. My muscles strain, and I feel this compelling need to kiss her.

What the fuck is wrong with me?

Mouse whimpers below me, her eyes sparkling with fear. I lean forward, spreading her legs wide, sinking deeper into her tight channel, hissing out in pleasure as she squeezes me so tightly the air in my lungs disappears. I settle just above her on my forearms. With both hands, I cradle her face, pulling it into mine. My lips settle onto hers as I slip another inch deeper. This time, when she whimpers, there's a tinge of pain to the noise and I kiss it away, my lips savoring hers. Her hands come up to the back of my head, holding me there.

I grunt into her mouth, feeling her tight pussy resist another inch of my swollen cock. I'm only halfway in and there is no fucking way that's all I'm giving her. My sweet mouse is going to take all nine inches of my length and then beg me for more.

"Xander" she cries beneath me, her eyes bleeding deeply into mine. I can feel her chest constrict beneath mine. I remind myself how fragile she is, like a delicate fucking flower. If I don't care for her, she will wilt away.

"Shhh, Mouse, it will only hurt for a few more moments," I lie, moving my lips from hers and down over her chin. I pepper kisses against her jaw and then down the slope of her throat. I press my lips firmly against her throbbing pulse and swivel my hips, slamming into her to the hilt in one thick motion.

Her body stiffens, and she cries out in pain. I know it hurt... Fuck, do I know. I can feel how tight she is, her body's resistance to my length, but she will adjust. My tiny mouse will survive.

I fist the sheets beside her head, afraid that if I touch her, I may bruise her. I want her so badly it consumes my every waking thought. There is no good or bad in this moment. There is simply Mouse and me, our bodies saying all the things neither of us ever could. I remain very still, beads of sweat form against my brow, and the tension in my body tightens.

I want to pound into her, to hear our flesh smack against each other's. I want to listen to her pants of pleasure and watch the flush of heat as it consumes her, but I won't... not yet.

Breaking you would be the biggest mistake... I remember the words I spoke to her last night, before she fell asleep in my arms. I move slowly, my strokes gentle, fluid, my hips move in a rolling motion, crashing into her like waves against the beach. I grit my teeth and up my pace slightly when I feel Mouse lifting her hips into mine, catching each thrust and giving it back to me.

"You feel like heaven, and you're as close as I'm ever going to get..." I press onward, meeting Mouse's tiny thrusts, her hands grip my skin, and tiny puffs of air leave her lungs. When her nails sink into my shoulder blades, tiny pricks of pain radiate down my spine, making me slam into her fiercely.

"Xander, I'm–I'm–coming..." she sighs, her blue eyes drifting closed. I feel heat blooming deep into my belly, the knot of pleasure unraveling with each and every stroke, pushing me closer and closer to an orgasm. Mouse's pussy flutters around me, her muscles tightening, her tiny nails giving me more pain. I relish in that pain. It festers deep inside me, and I elongate her orgasm, moving a hand between our bodies.

Two fingers find her engorged clit, begging to be played.

"Fuck, Mouse, I want you to come again. Squeeze my cock, make me come inside you." I pant the words into her ear. I lose control as her body obeys my command. Soft shudders of pleasure rip through her, and I push her shirt up, taking one of her pink puckered nipples into my mouth. I suck and flick the little bud, moving in and out of her furiously.

I'm not anywhere near my normal strokes, my normal need of pain mixed with pleasure, but I'm giving her everything I can without hurting her, and it's setting me on fire, igniting my soul, making something inside me snap.

My heart cracks, the darkness inside me pouring out of the damn muscle. I release her tit with a loud pop, biting the hardened nipple. Mouse whimpers in both pleasure and pain, and I move my hands down to her hips, holding her in place while I fuck us both into sweet oblivion. My grip is bruising, my pumps pushing us up the bed.

A tightening in my balls steals the air from my lungs, and Mouse's tiny nails sink deeper into my flesh with my hard strokes.

"Come inside me, Xander, come inside me... please..." she pleads, her words coated in pleasure. I gaze down at her, knowing it's not my son who is my biggest weakness. No, it's her, the tiny mouse with strawberry-blonde hair and big blue eyes.

She is a fucking weakness.

Falling forward, I lift her hips and press deeply into her channel, falling over the edge. Every inch of my body tenses. As pleasure fills my veins, a euphoria washes over me, and for a second, I can't breathe... or think. It's pure bliss.

I fill the condom with so much cum I worry it may spill out of the condom and inside her, but I can't be bothered with the thought. Not right then. Wrapping both hands under Mouse, I hold her tightly to my chest, and her heart beats to the same rhythm mine does. We're both panting, sweaty messes, and as my cock softens, the only thing I can think about is doing it all over again.

Because when I'm inside of Mouse, she owns me, completely. She owns the darkness; she owns the light. She fucking owns me, and it's terrifying... Looking down at her, I wonder if she realizes how much power she has over me. She's everything I can never have and still the only one I want right now.

"Are you hurt?" I murmur into her hair, slowly pulling out of her. She winces at the motion, and I've already gotten my answer.

"I'm not hurt... it just... it burns a little."

I shake my head, pulling her into my arms. A smile lingers on my lips as I take her tiny body against my chest and carry her into the bathroom.

A panicked look crosses her features and when I place her on the floor in the bathroom, her eyes drop down to my groin. I follow her gaze and realize why she's so panicked looking.

"I'm bleeding," she announces with embarrassment. She has no idea how much her innocence to all of this turns me on.

"No, Mouse, you're not. I didn't fuck you hard enough to make you bleed. It's just a little blood because I took your cherry..."

She wrinkles her nose at me as if she doesn't understand what I've said.

Oh, Mouse, what will I do with you?

I turn the shower on, making certain it's hot before I guide her into the spray of water.

"What's a cherry?" she questions, peering up at me, looking smaller than before. Everything about her brings out my protective instincts. I don't want to fucking hurt her... No, I want to protect her. I want to shield her from the storm, from the darkness that this world spreads. Lifting her by the chin, forcing her eyes to remain on mine, I answer her question.

"Your virginity. You bleed the first time you have sex."

Realization dawns on her, and she looks at me with shame in her eyes. "I'm sorry. I should've known that."

"It's okay, your nativity and misunderstanding of things only makes me want you more." My confession shocks even me, but I couldn't stop the words from coming out even if I wanted to.

"You want me?" she questions with amazement, as if she's shocked that I would still want her after taking her virginity. I suppose she assumed I'd toss her over my shoulder like garbage, but I can't.

I need her, so the darkness doesn't swallow me whole.

"Yes, again and again..." I lean down, feeling the heat of her breath on my lips, and I can't stop myself from kissing her. I can't... my lips press against hers and I swallow the gasp of surprise. She's inexperienced in kissing, her movements slow and unsure, but she's mine, and I'll teach her all she needs to know.

When I pull away, her pink lips are swollen, and I can tell she wants to say something...

"I... I think I'm..." I can feel the organ in my chest beat furiously, and I don't want to hear what she has to say... No. I won't let her ruin this moment between us.

"Get under the water, Mouse. We have places we need to go today, and I don't have the time to play with you all morning, so unless you want to get fucked again, shut up." The coldness of my words does exactly as I expected it to. She retreats inside herself, her eyes watering with unshed tears. Tears that I put there.

I'm doing it for you, Mouse, all for you.

11

*E*lla

Sex didn't make me feel any different. It just left a dull ache between my thighs and the evidence of my virginity being taken on the bed sheets. It was enjoyable though, and I was shocked at how gentle Xander was with me, though the slight sliver of roughness he gave me a taste of was something I wanted to explore, I wasn't ready to tell him that.

Xander dried me off from head to toe and walked me out into the bedroom. His coldness in the shower at the words I almost said saddened me. I was dumb for even considering telling him that I loved him... but I felt it deep inside my soul. I think he felt it, too, because he shut down completely. The darkness that surrounded him cloaked him and the man I shared an intense moment with disappeared.

"Get dressed. I had one of the maids get you some clothes, since I can't have you leaving the house in nothing more than my t-shirt."

My gaze swings to the bed and I'm surprised to see a pair of skinny jeans and a t-shirt, along with a pair of cotton panties and a white bra.

"Where are we going?" I ask, shivering as I put my clothes on.

Xander gawks at me, and desire pools in his gaze but he doesn't act on it. In fact, he dresses himself, putting on a suit that makes him look like a damn god. It's tailored to his body and as I look down at myself and what I'm wearing, I realize just how out of sorts I am.

"We are going wherever I say we're going," he answers, his tone tight. Tension coils deep inside him. He looks like he might snap at any given second.

He pulls a phone from his pocket, typing something out on it before pocketing it. Then he gets out his gun and places it in his holster. I wish more than anything that I had my phone... or anything that is mine, for that matter. My gaze drops down to my hands and, without a word, he walks out of the room.

What the hell?

I rush out the door behind him, my hands gripping onto his arm, stopping him mid-step. He swivels around on his feet so fast that I almost slam into him.

"Hey, why did you walk away without me? I just wanted to know—"

My words are cut off as Xander grips me by the throat. His touch is hot, his eyes are violent, warning me that in this moment he has all the control, and I understand why he's being this way now. All because of me... and the stupid need to tell him how I felt.

"Just because I showed you kindness and didn't fuck you until you bled to death doesn't mean were friends. It doesn't mean I have to tell you a fucking thing. You're still at my mercy, and if I want to fuck you into oblivion right this damn second, I will. I make the fucking rules... me!" he practically screams into my face.

My lips tremble, and my blood turns cold at the harshness of his voice.

I struggle to get out of his grip, but he squeezes ever so gently, just enough to make it hard to breathe. His fingers dig into my flesh, those same fingers having brought immense pleasure just hours ago.

"I'll make this very clear to you... I own you. I'll tell you what to wear, what to eat, who to talk to, and when you can piss. You're mine. But nothing we did today means shit. It was sex. That was fucking it. Don't get attached, and don't act like I give a fuck about you, because we both know that I don't. I could put a bullet right between your eyes, and it wouldn't affect me."

Tears stain my cheeks and as if his verbal abuse hasn't been enough, I add more to it with a question I know I won't like the answer to. "Why're you acting this way?"

"You think this is a fucking act?" His eyes darken, if that's even possible, and his fingers tighten around my neck. Black spots appear before my vision as the air in my lungs evaporates.

Panic creeps in, and I wonder if he might kill me. I grasp onto his wrist, trying to pull it away or at least loosen his grip, but he isn't budging, not even an inch.

"I should kill you right now. Get you out of my life for good."

I know he doesn't mean it. There is no way he wants me dead.

Yet, he is squeezing the life out of me, his actions betraying what I know he wants.

Our eyes are locked on each other, but I can't read him in this moment. I have no idea what he is thinking and a moment later, I don't care anymore. All I can think about is getting air into my lungs. I squeeze my eyes shut, wondering if this is it.

Will this be how I die?

As if he hears my words, he releases me. My lungs expand, sucking precious oxygen into my lungs. My legs give out under me and I slump to the floor, trying to get my erratic breathing under control. I gasp, my throat burns, but I am alive.

"Get up before I change my mind," he snaps, walking away from me. For a moment, I'm not sure if I can make myself get up. My whole body is shaking, and my legs feel like jelly. I'm terrified, and the last thing I want to do is get up and walk over to him like a puppy, but I know he means what he says.

Only when I realize Xander is almost at the end of the hallway do my limbs spring into action, giving me enough strength to get to a standing position. He stops to wait for me but doesn't say anything. I half jog over to him and only when I'm right next to him does he continue walking forward, each step full of purpose.

"Don't talk to me unless I speak to you. Don't talk to anyone else at all. Don't even look at anyone. Just keep your mouth shut and your eyes on the floor. Do exactly what I tell you to or I promise you, you will pay dearly."

A shudder runs through my spine at the coldness of his words. I keep my eyes trained to the floor as we walk through the house and out the front door. I take in a deep breath as soon as we are outside, realizing that I haven't had a breath of fresh air in days, but it feels more like weeks. And suddenly, I realize I don't even know what day it is.

We walk down a set of stairs, and up to a limousine where one of the guards is already holding open the door for us. Xander gets in without looking at me and I follow closely behind him. The door closes, leaving Xander and me in the small confined space alone.

The tension between us is thick, stifling even, making it hard enough to breathe. I'm scared to even look at him right now, but I still don't dare to sneak a peek at him. Of course, he is looking at me, I can feel his heated gaze on my skin. Clearly, he is still mad, and I'm confused. I haven't really done anything.

Instead of saying something to me, he gets his phone out of his pocket and moves his fingers over the screen swiftly. Then he puts it to his ear.

"Is the plane ready?"

Plane? Where exactly are we going that we need to take a plane?

"Great... we will be there momentarily. I want to be in the air within the next hour." I gulp and shift uncomfortably. I hate flying. More than hate. I'm freaking terrified of it. I watch as he hangs up the phone and then types out something. I lift my gaze slightly and wonder if he feels bad for treating me the way he did.

"I..." I start to apologize, but when I meet Xander's eyes, I clam up. His eyes are murderous, and the grip he has on his phone is hard.

"If you were half as smart as you act, you'd shut your fucking mouth right now. I'm barely holding on to my temper, and I can promise you, it's not something you want to test."

A profound pain radiates through my chest. I swallow my apology down, deciding that he doesn't deserve it. I don't move or say a single thing for the rest of the drive. When the car stops and the door opens, Xander gets out, and I follow behind him, even though I don't want to. As soon as my feet hit the hard ground, he's on me.

"If you run from me at any point in time, I will put a bullet in you. Got it?"

I nod my head profusely, and he backs up. I don't believe he'll shoot me if I run, but I do know he'll hurt me. I watch him walk up the small metal staircase to the plane, and I have to force my legs to walk up behind him. My hand grips onto the rail so tightly my knuckles turn white.

When I finally make it to the top, I'm dizzy and I feel like throwing up already. I take a few steps into the plane before I look up. I expect Xander to glare at me and yell for me to hurry up. Instead, I see Keira jumping up from one of the huge leather seats. She heads straight for me with a wide smile on her face, and I just stand there motionlessly.

She slams into me and wraps her arms around me, pulling me in for a big hug like we are old friends who haven't seen each other in years. Even though I've only met this girl once and exchanged a few words with her, I already like her. I like her kindness and right now, I like her hug. The sweet gesture warms my heart and makes me feel a little less scared.

I lean my head onto her shoulder and wrap my arms around her, embracing her touch.

"Are you okay? Do you need anything?" she whispers into my hair, and I almost start to cry. Her voice is so kind, so calm. I want to tell her everything, even though I don't know her at all.

"I'm okay, I'm just scared of flying." I don't know why that's all I'm telling her right now. Shouldn't I be asking her for help? Asking her to help me get away from Xander? I know I could ask her for help, and she'd help me, but being this close to finding my sister, I'm not so sure it's worth it.

"Keira, get your hands off my property," Xander yells from the back of the plane, interrupting my train of thought.

"She is not your property!" Keira shouts, fire blazing in her eyes. I get the feeling she doesn't like Xander just from the dirty look she's giving him.

"Keira, just stay out of it. Come and sit down, baby." Xander's brother comes up to us, grabbing his wife by the arms very gently while ushering her to the seat beside him.

How did Xander's brother end up so different than him? It's like they're two different people. I wonder how Keira met Damon and if he was different, more like his brother, before they got together. I remind myself to ask Keira later all of these questions. But for now, I'll just keep my mouth shut.

I feel like I'm doing the walk of shame as I step farther into the plane and walk up to where Xander took a seat. It's all the way in the back of the plane and farthest away from where Keira is sitting. I hate how far away from them we are, and I desperately want to turn on my heels and walk in the opposite direction.

"Sit," Xander orders and I know he is furious with me by his tone alone. I haven't dared to look him in the eyes. Only when I sit down on the seat across from him do I finally look up to meet his gaze. I don't know what I'm more scared of at this moment... him or the flight.

Both could easily be the end of me. I place my shaking hands in my lap and wait for him to say something else, anything really at this point. Tears fill my eyes, and I can't stop them from coming. Today was perfect until I opened my mouth to tell him that I thought maybe I loved him. Thinking on it now, it was such a stupid thing to even consider saying.

I swipe at my eyes with the back of my hands. I want to ask him why he's so angry over words that I never fully said, but I bite my tongue. The fear of the unknown stops me. I sit in silence, buckling my lap belt before staring at my hands, which I'm nervous fiddling around with.

Once the plane starts moving, however, my fear of the flight overcomes my fear of Xander. My head snaps up to him, meeting his eyes. I open my mouth to say something, but he shakes his head. My chest is heaving, and I look out the window to see trees whizzing by. We are about to take off and I am in full on panic mode. I look back at Xander, my fearful expression making his death glare morph into curiosity.

"What the fuck is wrong with you?" he asks low enough so only I can hear him, his hands gripping the arm rests.

"I'm scared of flying," I admit, my voice low and shaky. I don't dare look up at him. I feel the plane rise into the air, and I squeeze my eyes shut. Trying to calm my erratic breathing, I hope I'm not going to hyperventilate. I hear Xander unbuckle his lap belt, and I open my eyes to find him standing beside me. Then he leans down and unbuckles me from my seat.

"What...?" I don't finish my question, remembering what happened last time I asked something. Xander just grabs me by the arm and pulls me from my seat like I'm a rag doll. He drags me along with him, and I nearly trip three times before we make it to the back of the plane. A door opens, and Xander pulls me in, before closing us inside. I look around the room, noticing that this is a small bedroom.

Why are we in a bedroom? The sound of Xander undoing his belt and unzipping his pants fills the room. I blanch, shaking my head slightly as I peer up at him. He has an evil glint in his eyes. I step backward, trying to put some distance between us, but he's having none of that. He grips me by the arm, pulling me into his chest, his hardened cock poking me in the belly.

"I... I'm too sore..." I'm praying for mercy, all while knowing I won't be getting any, at least not today. Xander is showing me the side of him that everyone else gets. He's showing me that if I get too close, he'll bite, much like a cornered animal.

"I told you not to touch or talk to anybody. I told you not to speak to me unless you are spoken to. I told you to follow my fucking rules or you will pay dearly. You didn't make it twenty minutes before breaking every single one of those rules, and I'm starting to think you aren't taking me serious?"

He leans in real close, his nose nearly touching mine. I can feel the danger oozing out of him and my first instinct is to run, hide, and protect myself from the evil man before me. But I don't. I can't. If I want to understand him, then I have to face him, the beast, the darkness.

"No, I am, but I don't understand why you're so mad? I didn't do anything. Everything was fine until I brought up my feelings in the shower."

"Your feelings don't mean shit to me." He sits down on the edge of the bed, taking me with him. He grabs me by the shoulder, his fingers pressing harshly into my skin, causing me to whimper. He pushes me down to the floor and onto my knees before him and it's then that I realize exactly what he wants.

I actually calm down a bit, knowing that this is something I can do. I can give him pleasure this way. I peek up at him, as I push a couple strands of hair behind my ear. I take his length into my hand and feel its weight. My thumb rubs across the silky-smooth tip and over the slit.

"Your mouth, Mouse. I want your fucking mouth. Don't use your teeth, and don't bite me. Otherwise, you won't like what happens," he hisses, weaving his hands into my hair, guiding me to his length. I open my mouth and let him slide over my tongue as far as he can go before making me gag.

I close my lips around him and start sucking, alternating between hard and soft sucks. A low groan fills my ears, and I keep sucking and swirling my tongue at his tip. I pull out a little and stroke him with my hand, just like I did last time.

Then I take him as deep as I can again, but this time, he won't let me go back. The hand in my hair tightens and he holds my head in place with it. Instead of sliding back out, he pushes his penis to the back of my throat, making me gag. My eyes water, and I look up at him, pleading with him to stop.

"Just relax your throat, breathe in through your nose, and swallow with every stroke." He takes his other hand and places it against my cheek, stroking it with his knuckles. His touch is comforting, and he looks down at me with the adoration in his eyes instead of fury like earlier.

I do as he tells me, swallowing around his length as he moves in and out of my mouth deeply. I still gag, but it becomes more bearable with each stroke. Tears slip from my eyes as he uses my mouth just like he would my body.

I watch pleasure contort in his features, and his hips thrust harder, faster. I can barely breathe through his movements, but I'm still watching him take from me, watching him use me. It turns me on. My pussy clenches, and though it's sore, I know that if Xander touched me right now, it would turn into molten lava.

"You're mine, Mouse... mine..." He slams all the way to the back of my throat, his grip tightening as he comes harshly, his teeth clenched, and his eyes closed. I swallow the salty release down, swirling my tongue across his slit one last time as he pulls out of my mouth. When his eyes finally open, there's a calmness to the storm that was brewing before.

He helps me to my feet and traces a knuckle against my jaw before dressing himself.

"If you don't want me to treat you like this again, then don't pretend there is anything more than sex between us. I don't want to hear about your feelings. I don't want to hear about anything personal. I just want your pleasure, and maybe a little bit of your pain. Do you understand me?"

I lick my lips and nod my head.

"Good, now let's go back to our seats." He opens the door, and I walk back to my seat, my eyes trained to the floor. I hope Keira doesn't think differently of me now. I understood before why he was so angry, why he had so much fire in his eyes, but I get it much more now that he's spoken to me.

I see right through the facade of pain and anger.

The man who claims to be unlovable is falling for me, just as I am him, and there's nothing quite as terrifying as being completely exposed and at the mercy of another human being.

12

$\mathcal{X}$ander

WHEN WE LAND IN VEGAS, I'm much calmer. Which probably has something to do with the amazing blowjob Mouse gave me earlier and the fact that she's actually listened to me for the remainder of the flight.

Still, guilt consumes me every time I look at her. I didn't want to hurt her, but I needed her to know how serious I was about her feelings for me. She can't know how consumed with need I am for her because she'll only use it against me.

She already knows I don't want to hurt her, but hopefully, I've set her straight with this whole... 'I think I *love* you' bullshit. She doesn't know the first thing about love, or all it entails... what it means to be with a man like me. I watched my mother love my father for years, and it never turned out well for her. He beat her, stripped her bare, and turned her against her children. Love ruined my mother. It destroyed her, and I couldn't let Mouse make the same mistake.

My eyes dart to Keira and my brother. They seem so happy, so in love, and parts of me wish I could have the same kind of life they do. But I'm not stupid enough to hope for something like that. I can never have what they have, because I'm not like Damon. He married Keira to save her from my wrath. He protected her. He toned his darkness down.

He let go of his pain for his wife, but I don't know that I'm capable of doing that. Not when my enemies would be chomping at the bit to put a bullet in her head.

Love isn't an option for me, not even close. I need to remain the dark, calloused boss that I am. I shake the silly thoughts away as Damon and Keira exit the plane first. I wait a few moments before I follow with Mouse closely by my side.

"Remember the rules." I leave the threat unspoken but we both know it's there. Mouse nods, her eyes trained on the floor. *Good girl.*

We all pile into the limo waiting for us on the landing strip. It can easily seat eight people but with the uncomfortable silence between us, it suddenly feels too small. Keira is staring daggers at me, making me smile on the inside. On the outside, I show no emotion whatsoever, just like I've learned to do.

"You are aware she is a human, right?" Keira sneers, completely ignoring anything my brother said to her. She's putting her nose into something it doesn't belong in and obviously, I need to make sure she understands that.

"I'm sure you're more than aware that I don't give a fuck what you have to say. After all, if it weren't for my brother, you'd be dead, too."

Mouse seems to gasp beside me, but Keira's looking at me with murder in her eyes, not fear. I smirk like the bastard I am.

"Xander, knock it the fuck off." Damon snarls, grabbing onto Keira's hands as if he already knows what she wants to do to me. I bet if I gave her a gun, she'd pull the trigger. She'd be smart, too. I killed her brother. An eye for an eye, right?

"He can't treat her like that, Damon. It's clear he is hurting her. Look at her." I can see the conflict in Damon's eyes at Keira's words. He wants to please his wife, but he knows better than to get into my business.

"She's none of our concern." The coldness in Damon's voice shocks even me. Usually, he speaks to Keira so kindly, and with love, but right now, I can tell he's clearly pissed.

Mouse remains quiet, with her gaze on her hands.

"I'm not hurting her. I haven't done a fucking thing to her. I've merely asked her to follow my fucking directions."

Keira's eyes widen. "You are aware her name isn't Mouse, right? It's Ella. Fucking Ella. She has a name, Xander. She has feelings, and she is a damn human, not your property. I will not let you hurt her."

I'd never considered Mouse's name to be Ella but looking at her, it seems to fit her. Sweet, naive, a princess. Keira's words spark a fire deep inside me. She's accusing me of hurting Mouse, and while I haven't been very kind to her, I haven't truly hurt her, not like I know I should. Hell, I'm here looking for Mouse's sister, all with the intention of killing my father. I've never done such a thing for someone.

"Don't accuse me of shit you have no proof of... not that it would matter anyway. If I wanted to snap her neck right fucking here, right now, it wouldn't matter. There wouldn't be a damn thing you could do about it, would there?" I dart an eyebrow up in question, knowing damn well there is nothing she can do.

"Xander..." There's a warning to Damon's voice, and I have half a mind to tell him to get back on the plane and go home with his pain in the ass wife, but revenge against our father is half his, so I bite my tongue this once.

The limo rolls to a stop, and I peer out the window, realizing we have arrived at the hotel.

"Let's go to our rooms and then meet for dinner in an hour's time."

Damon nods, taking Keira's hand in his. We all exit the limo at once, and I pull Mouse into my body as soon as we step outside. "We need to get invited to this auction, and I know just the guy who will let us in, but it would be better if we are all seen together. So, Keira, maybe you could stop being such a raging bitch and..." My voice trails off at the murderous rage appearing in my brother's eyes.

"She's my fucking wife." Damon looks like he is about to punch me in the face, so I decide to leave it at that and walk away with a smirk, guiding Mouse toward the elevator. Mouse's eyes are wide and full of wonder as she looks at every single little thing, as if she's a little kid in a candy store for the very first time.

She looks happy, and her smile widens. Well, that is until she sees me.

"I'm sorry..." she mutters beneath her breath, and I usher us into the elevator, wanting to tell her she has no reason to be sorry... not for this.

"Don't be sorry, Mouse. I enjoy seeing your smile," I whisper, my hand against the small of her back as more people pile into the elevator. I pull her as closely against my body as I can and watch the numbers tick upward, stopping here and there to drop people off.

When we reach the very top floor, we get off and I enter a special code into the door, opening it and ushering Mouse inside. Our luggage has already been brought up and is waiting for us at the door. I roll it to the bedroom with Mouse following me closely. She looks like she is afraid of touching anything or stepping onto something she isn't supposed to. Obviously, she's not used to staying in five-star hotels.

I get out Mouse's dress and lay it down on the king-sized bed. When I turn around, I nearly run into her, my hands grasping onto her arms. She looks up at me through light brown lashes, her big blue eyes full of unknown emotions.

"Do you think we will really find her?"

I release her and turn around and walk toward the floor-to-ceiling windows that overlook the Strip.

I need a fucking drink in order to deal with all of this. My own emotions are conflicting with the things I must do. I know letting Mouse in will only hurt her, but the idea of actually having her fascinates me. I want to throttle her and make sweet, sweet love to her all at once.

"I don't know, Mouse." I turn to face her, seeing the sadness flicker in her blue depths. I want to remove that sadness and replace it with pleasure, desire, need, anything but goddamn sadness.

"We need to get ready for dinner. Would you like to join me for a shower?" I start to strip out of my suit, undoing the cuffs and my belt, shucking my shirt, pants, and shoes to the floor. I remove every single piece of clothing, feeling her eyes on me. As soon as I start walking toward the bathroom, she stands undressing herself as she follows me, leaving a trail of clothing behind her. Turning the shower on and all the way to hot, I grab her hand and tug her inside with me, closing the glass door behind us.

When I turn around, she's turned away from me with her face directly under the water. I take the opportunity to take in every inch of her perfect ass, as well the slope of her back, and her long strawberry-blonde hair that hangs down it. I envision myself wrapping my hands in her hair and fucking her. My eyes move down to her ass again.

Fuck, I'll claim her there soon, too. Every part I can weasel myself into, I will claim. But for right now, I want to return the favor and give her the same fucking pleasure she gave me earlier. Licking my lips, I take a step forward, stopping only once I've pressed my hard front against the curve of her back. Her skin is soft, and I want to mark her skin, make it known that she belongs to me and only me.

"I want to taste you, Mouse." I press my lips against the side of her neck, alternating between sucking and kissing. She softly whimpers, tilting her head, exposing more of her neck to me. And like a man starved of food, I ravage her, turning her around in my arms, while backing up to press her back against the tile. I blaze a trail of hot kisses across her collarbone and down between her tits, rolling her pink puckered nipples between my fingers.

My lips travel lower, over her smooth belly, and to each hip, which I bite tenderly. Another soft whimper of pleasure escapes her pink lips as I do this, and I slowly drop down to my knees on the floor before her. Her hands make their way into my hair, and she peers down at me. She looks like a goddamn angel, and fuck, I'll be damned if I don't want to fuck the good right out of her. Placing a soft kiss against her mound, I slide the tip of my tongue between her folds, very slowly, before hooking both of her legs over my shoulders.

She slides down the wall with a yelp, but I catch her ass in my hands, my fingers messaging the soft flesh.

"I'll always catch you if you fall," I murmur into her softness, pressing my lips over her clit. I move my hands up, to her thighs, spreading her wider, until I see her pretty pink pussy beckoning me forward.

I lick my lips and dive in, licking her from top to bottom. She melts in my fucking hands, and I feel my cock harden when her fingers grip onto my hair painfully.

"Hurt me, Mouse. Hurt me like I hurt you," I growl against her pussy, and her moan of pleasure vibrates through the fucking walls of the bathroom. I know I have to hear that sound again. I feast on her like she is my last meal, licking and sucking her clit furiously. Mouse starts panting and I suck harder, flicking the tip of my tongue all while continuing to suck.

I feel my muscles burning, my need to be inside her nearly consuming me, but I push the fucking thought down as I feel her fingers sink into my scalp. Her nails are nothing, but they dig into the skin, causing a sting of pain and pleasure to course through my veins.

"Come for me, Mouse, come all over my fucking tongue," I demand.

She wiggles her ass in my hands as if she's trying to get away, and I smile, knowing there is nowhere for her to go.

"I... Xander... I'm..." She gasps, her movements frantic, and her hips thrust upward, grinding her pussy into my face. I move from her clit to her entrance right as she goes off, my tongue swirling around inside her tight little hole as her sweet cream gushes all over my tongue.

"Mmmm..." I moan between her folds. "You taste so fucking delicious. Like a find fucking wine, I think you taste better every time I dip my tongue inside you."

I lick her from ass to clit a few more times before placing her back on her feet. Her knees seem to buckle beneath her, and she places a hand on my shoulder to steady herself.

"You're really good... at that." She giggles, and it's the cutest fucking sound I've ever heard. I take in her pinked cheeks and her big blue eyes that have this sated look to them. She looks relaxed and thank fuck, because I don't know what the hell is going to happen at this auction tonight. I don't know if Mouse's sister is even alive still, but I hope so.

I really fucking do, because I want to make her happy even after everything. I still want her to be happy. I have no fucking clue how, but I'll try. I want to keep that beautiful smile of hers on her face as long as I can.

"I've got lots and lots of practice." I wink and start washing us both.

"Does it bother you that I'm not as experienced as you?" she asks as I wash her hair, gently massaging her scalp.

"Not a single bit. Knowing I'll be your first everything is very... satisfying." My honesty to her question surprises me. The more I'm around her, the more I want to tell her. I want to tell her about my past, about what I want for my future.

Fuck. I put up this front. I tell myself I have to be this hardened criminal only to hate myself later for hurting her. Like before we got on the plane. I hurt her. I could see it in her eyes, the sadness, the anger, and fear. How long can I keep this up with her?

The thought of being that man to her kills me. As I rinse her hair, I think about the fact that I could do this for her every single day. I could keep her as mine, and mine only. I've already told her she can never leave. It would be so easy to do.

"I want to keep you, Mouse," I whisper into her ear.

Her eyes open instantly, shock, and something else reflecting in her depths. "Keep? As in like property? Or keep as in something more?"

I smirk. "Maybe a little bit of both. I don't really know. All I know is that I don't want to have to hurt you, and I don't think I can ever let you go, so maybe we can come to a compromise... an agreement." I stumble over my words nervously, like I'm fifteen again and asking some fucking chick out on a date.

Mouse stares at me for a long moment, saying nothing. Then she pushes up onto the tips of her toes, sliding her slick body against mine.

She presses her lips against mine softly. "I like you, Xander, but I really like you when you're the man you are now. When you drop the act and stop pretending that you are a monster. We all have a little bit of darkness inside us, but that doesn't mean it has to define us."

"I'm not pretending to be a monster, I know I am. And there isn't just a little bit of darkness inside of me. There is a whole fucking truck load. It swallows up all of the good. It taints every fucking inch of my heart, and I can't be the man that I am with you right now... not when we are out there. I can never show anybody this side of me. I shouldn't even have shown it to you." Fuck, I shouldn't have.

"But you did, and now that I've seen this part of you, I'm not sure I can ever forget it exists." Her tiny hands cup my cheeks, and I lean into her touch, reveling in it. It's warm and it calms the fucking storm inside me.

Staring into my eyes, she continues, "You might think you're past saving, but I don't think so. I just think you haven't found the one single person willing to go through heaven and hell for you."

My heart thuds against my ribs, and I want to tell her I have... I really fucking do, but I can't. Not yet. I choke down all the feelings threatening to escape me and clench my fists at my side. I feel sick, knowing I have to become him, but it has to be done...

"We really need to get ready." I change the subject, pulling out of her touch, and she gives me a knowing smile. My mouse sees right through the bullshit and if that's not the scariest fucking thing ever, then I don't know what is.

I rinse all the soap out of her hair before I turn the shower off and step out to grab two towels. I wrap her up in a large one and dry her hair with a smaller one before leading her back into the bedroom. I sling one towel over my shoulder.

"I got you this dress for tonight." I unzip the plastic bag it's in and hold it up.

Her eyes go wide as she takes in the short red dress. The fabric is soft, but I know for a fact it will hug every single inch of her curves.

"Xander, you didn't have to." She smiles, running her fingers over the material.

"I know I didn't, but I wanted to. Plus, the place we are going is not really a skinny jeans and sneakers kind of place." I put the dress down on the bed and pluck the matching red thong and strapless bra from within the same bag.

She nibbles on her bottom lip, spotting the scrap of fabric. Fuck, would I love to know what she's thinking.

"Get dressed, Mouse. Oh, and I look forward to seeing you in that thong later." I wink and then press a kiss to her lips before pulling away, my cock stiffer than hell, reminding me of how much not only my heart wants her but my body, too.

Mine. All fucking mine.

13

Ella

I GLARE at the four-inch heels Xander is expecting me to wear tonight. I can't figure out how I'm going to manage walking in them without breaking my ankle or embarrassing him.

"Remember what you said earlier in the shower about you always catching me?"

Xander looks up from buttoning his shirt. "Yes, of course."

"Well, I hope you meant it, because I will probably do a lot of falling in these." I slip into the black heels with red soles and take a few unsteady steps. They are much more comfortable than I expected them to be, but it still takes me a few rounds of walking around the room before I start to look like a person walking instead of a newborn fawn.

"I'm sure you'll manage, Mouse. You ready?"

I take another look at myself in the mirror. The dress is absolutely stunning and fits me like a glove. I blow dried my hair and straightened it, then did some light makeup. I didn't want to do something that was too eye catching. My wrists are still an angry red-looking mess, and I really wish I had something to cover them up.

I can't imagine what everyone will think when they see them.

Xander comes up behind me, looking at my reflection in the mirror. "You look beautiful, and those will eventually heal." He makes reference to my wrists as if he can read my mind. "Don't worry about what everyone else thinks, Mouse. They don't know your story."

He has no idea how much his words mean to me, no idea at all.

"And while I'd love nothing more than to stay in this room all evening with you, we really need to go now. Damon and Keira are waiting downstairs for us."

I nod and smile as he walks us to the door. Xander grabs the knob but doesn't open it right away, and I wonder what he's thinking.

"Remember what I told you. I can't be like this out there. Not tonight or any other time we're doing business. You get that, right?" I can hear the sincerity in his voice.

"Yes," I answer. He opens the door for me, and I walk across the threshold, almost falling over my own feet. Xander grabs my arm to steady me before he holds out his arm for me to loop mine under.

"Just hold on to me and remember the rules. Everything I told you yesterday you have to do... especially today. There are some really bad people, far worse than me, Mouse, and believe me when I tell you, you don't want to draw their attention."

My eyes widen slightly. "I understand, Xander," I assure him with a smile, and we get into the elevator and head down to the lobby. Damon and Keira are already waiting for us at the elevator when we exit. When I see Keira, I smile, and she smiles back, her smile fading when she notices the dirty look Xander is giving her.

She wrinkles her nose at him, and I almost start laughing. My gaze roams over Keira. She's wearing a royal blue, off-the-shoulder cocktail dress that ends right above her knee. She looks so stunning that I forget I'm not supposed to actually be looking at her.

Quickly, I avert my eyes to the floor and tighten my grip on Xander's arm. Nervous butterflies explode inside my belly. I'm a bundle of nerves right now. The thought of possibly finding my sister excites me and terrifies me all at once.

It's been forever since I've seen her or hugged her, and I can't wait to just be in the same room as her again. My thoughts are interrupted as we walk outside where the limo is already waiting for us. The door is held open by one of Xander's men, as always. I climb in very slowly, sliding across the leather seats. Xander gets in behind me, his fingers splaying across my back, as if he is showing ownership of me without really saying it.

His touch is gentle, and I want to sink into it. He pulls me into his side but doesn't say anything to me. Then again, he doesn't have to... his actions assure me that he cares. He and Damon discuss some business matters about their father on the way to the restaurant. I look out the window, trying to take everything in, but there is just way too much going on.

Every building we pass has lights that blind me. Hundreds of people walk down the sidewalks, some wearing ridiculous outfits, some wearing hardly anything at all. It's a sight to see, that is for sure.

The limo rolls to a stop along the curb in front of the restaurant. Seconds later, the door opens, and we get out. I hold my breath, praying I don't fall and break my ankle or, even worse, embrace Xander. I sigh in relief when my pointed heels stick firmly to the ground. I'm careful not to look around, even though I'm curious to know where we're eating and what the place looks like. Xander ushers us all inside, and out of the corner of my eye, I see the hottest girl. She doesn't even ask who we are or what table we want. Instead, she says, "Follow me, please," and leads the way. We walk for what seems like an eternity before she seats us. When she kindly asks us what we would like to drink, Xander orders without looking at her.

"Whisky neat for me, and water for her."

I don't have to look up to see who is snorting angrily across the table. I wish he would just let me tell Damon and Keira about us. Why can't they not know? What's the harm in his brother knowing about us? Does he think it will make him look weak? Or does he want to hide me from them?

"Whiskey as well, and whatever she would like," Damon announces.

I lift my gaze to Keira and see the fire flickering in her eyes. She's really angry, like really angry, and for the first time ever, I wonder what the story between them is. I remember Xander saying something about her dying if Damon hadn't married her in one of their previous sparring matches. I guess that would make me angry, too, but she seems to have it out for Xander in the worst way.

"I'll take a water as well." She tries to keep her voice calm but her tone all but says she is pissed. I unravel my napkin and settle it into my lap.

I feel Xander's hand land on my thigh beneath the table, and I almost gasp at his touch. I peek a glance at him, and pleasure zings straight through me and into my core when I see the desire pooling in his gaze.

The hostess walks away, mumbling something about how our waitress will be with us shortly but no one says anything.

"Should I try and stab you again?" Keira growls, her hands balled into tiny little fists.

"Didn't work out to well for you the first time, if I remember?" Xander doesn't even blink.

Damon seems annoyed with both of them, a frustrated sigh expelling from his lungs. "Keira, you're not stabbing my brother. Xander, you're not going to hurt my wife. Can't you two just get along?"

"Nope," they both say in unison. Their sparring match is giving me whiplash. Our waitress shows up a moment later with our drinks sitting them in front of each of us. She starts rambling on about the daily specials, but I don't think anybody is listening to a word she is saying. The tension is thick, and Damon reaches for his glass immediately, downing half of it within seconds.

"I'll be needing at least five more of these," he tells the waitress, who looks at him with wide eyes. Silence settles upon the table while Xander and Keira continue to stare at each other with anger resonating in their eyes.

"Are we ready to order?" The waitress somehow gets the words out, and I know I won't get a chance to order, so instead, I reach for my glass of water, taking a small sip.

"I'll take a King Prime Rib, and she'll take a Queen," Xander orders without even blinking, his gaze still firmly on Keira.

The waitress moves her eyes to Keira, who orders next, "I'll take an order of pineapple, mashed potatoes and gravy, and a chicken breast smothered in onions and mushrooms."

I blink at her order. It's so bizarre, almost as if she's...

"Don't mind her, she's pregnant." Damon laughs, all but taking the words out of my mouth. "And I'll have a King Prime Rib as well."

The waitress scurries away, leaving us all alone once again. I smile and mouth a congratulations at Keira from across the table. I feel Xander pull his hand away and, out of the corner of my eye, I see him reach for something with that same hand in his suit pocket. I quickly realize it's the pill bottle holding my antibiotics. He pops the top on the bottle and hands me one without saying a word. I take it from him without a word and put it into my mouth, swallowing it down with a sip of water.

"Are you fucking kidding me?" Keira all but yells.

Damon leans into her and whispers something in her ear, but that only seems to make her more livid. "No, I will not stop. Do you not see what your brother is doing to that poor girl? Are you drugging her? Seriously, Xander? You've ruined a lot of people's lives. Almost mine, and your brother's, and now you want to ruin hers, too."

My stomach clenches at her words. She doesn't know Xander, not like I do, and maybe that's half the problem.

My eyes move from Keira and back to Xander. His jaw is clenched, and he grips the glass of whiskey in his hands so tightly I worry the glass will crack. To most, he would seem unfazed by her words, but I know him better than that and there is no way I can just sit here and not stick up for him. Consequences be damned... *I won't let her think any worse of him than she already does. Yes, he's an evil man, but there is goodness inside him. I know this because I am still alive.*

"It's not like that, Keira. He's not drugging me."

Keira laughs, but it's not a funny kind of laugh. "Oh, joy, he's convinced you that he's not some sick son of a bitch that gets off on hurting others."

"Keira," Damon scolds, slamming his fist down on the table, startling both Keira and me. Tears begin to well in her brown eyes, and I want to reach out and hug her just like she did me the last time I was scared. Damon mutters, "Fuck," under his breath before he pulls her chair across the floor, bringing her body closer to his.

"Don't bother, brother. If she wants to think the worst of me, she can. She doesn't know me. Not really. And I can't really blame her for being angry. I did, after all, kill her brother and threaten to kill her as well, so she does have a right to think horribly of me." The smile Xander gives his brother sends shivers down my spine. He's only saying these things to play up the image he wants people to see. Anything less and he'd be considered weak.

"He didn't deserve to die, and you know it." She spits the words at him.

The waitress arrives then, five glasses of whiskey on her small tray. She places them on the table and walks away once more. I wonder if she can sense the hostility wafting from our table.

"Believe that all you want, but I don't make a habit of killing people who don't deserve it. Your brother stole from me... so he paid with his life." Xander's tone is all matter-of-fact like, and as he takes a gulp of his whiskey, his eyes slowly move from Keira and to me. I sizzle under his heated gaze.

"Whatever, Xander. You'll never apologize for anything because you have no heart. You don't know what it's like to lose someone you love. But someday it will happen to you, and when it does, I hope it hurts. I hope it hurts so bad it breaks your black soul in two."

Keira shoves from her chair, wiping at the stray tears that stain her cheeks. She walks away from table and out of the room completely. Damon looks conflicted, but he gets up from the table, chasing after her.

Xander downs the rest of his whiskey, slamming the glass down onto the table. I don't dare say a word. I'm not dumb enough to do that.

"See, Mouse... I'm nothing but a monster. An evil bastard with a black soul." He reaches for another glass of whiskey, and tears sting my eyes.

Xander and I have crossed a line. Somewhere, somehow, we've decided we care for each other, and it hurts me more than I want to admit that he lets others think so harshly of him. Yes, he's a monster but he has it in him to do better. If only more people believed in that part of him, maybe, just maybe, he would make better choices.

"You aren't... we both know that." I want to throw my arms around his neck and pull him into my embrace so badly it hurts. I want to hug and kiss him, take his pain and self-doubt away... and I do just that. I scan the room we are in; no one can see us right now. I close the short distance between Xander and me, seeing anger simmering in his dark eyes, but I don't care.

"Consequences be damned, Xander, you're worthy of being loved. Even if you don't think so." My lips press against his. He tastes like whiskey and sin. At first, he does nothing, as if he is in shock but as soon as he realizes I've kissed him, his fingers weave into my hair, pulling me closer. I gasp as his tongue pushes into my mouth and my hands grip onto the front of his suit. I never want this kiss to end... but way too soon, it does. Xander releases me, and I slip back into my seat, my lips swollen, and my mind reeling with all the different things I want him to do to me.

Damon and Keira return after a few minutes, and Keira seems to be in a much better mood. About the same time they come back, dinner is being served. We eat in silence for a few minutes, and I stuff my face, the food melting on my tongue with every bite I take. I'm slightly startled when Damon suddenly clears his throat to get our attention.

"Here comes our guy," he says under his breath, looking past Xander to someone.

"I can't believe my eyes. The Rossi brothers are back together again." I keep my eyes trained on my plate, trying not to look at the face connected to the creepy voice.

"Benny, it has been a while, hasn't it, old friend?" Damon greets him, standing to shake his hand. I really hope they are not actually friends. "This is Keira, my wife."

"Damon Rossi a married man... who would have thought? Very nice to meet you." I watch him walk around to our side of the table, an uneasy feeling festering in my gut. "Xander, it's been awhile since I've seen you."

"Benny, you know how business goes." He stands to shake hands just as Damon did.

"And who might this beautiful creature be?" Benny asks curiously, and I can feel his eyes on me. I bite the inside of my cheek, hating the way this situation makes me feel.

Xander sits back down and shrugs nonchalantly. "Just something to play with when I'm not working."

It's like I'm a prized piece of meat or something.

"Quite the toy you have." I can hear the interest in his voice, and it's sickening.

"I've grown rather tired of this toy. I think I might buy a new one soon." Xander sounds bored and completely unattached. And even though I know he is just acting this way, it still hurts to hear him talk like this about me.

"You're in luck, old friend. There is an event later tonight where you can do just that."

Hope settles deep in my belly. Violet might be there. I could see my sister again, tonight even. Benny hands Xander something that he grabs from the inside pocket of his suit jacket.

"You'll need these to get in. I've seen the lineup, and they're offering some exquisite merchandise tonight. If this is your type, there is one who looks a lot like her."

It takes everything in me to remain in my seat. I want to jump up and demand him to bring me there right now, but I know that wouldn't help me or Violet.

"Is that so? Well, I guess I'll have to go and see for myself." Xander slides the invites into his jacket, and I hope like hell this Benny creep is going to leave now.

Instead, he walks around my chair, standing directly behind me. "I'll take this one off your hands if you end up buying something new tonight."

I ball my hands into fists so tightly that my nails dig painfully into my palm.

"I'm not quite done with her yet, but I'll keep you in mind when I am." I can hear the annoyance mixed with anger in Xander's voice even though he is trying to hide it. Apparently, Benny does not.

"How much do you want for her?" He places one hand on the table and leans into my body, lifting his other hand to reach for my cheek. I want to shy away, run to the farthest corner I can to stop him from touching me, but I can't. Doing so would draw attention to us.

He gets about half an inch away from touching my skin before Xander moves with superhuman speed. He is so fast that I don't really understand what's happening... until it's already done. I watch with shock swirling deep in my belly as he slams his fist harshly onto Benny's hand, standing up hastily and causing the chair to fall to the floor behind him. I feel Xander's hands on me and before I can even grasp what is happening, he's pulling me to my feet, bringing me in to his side.

Benny cries out in pain and when I look down and see blood gushing from his hand onto the white table cloth, I notice a fork sticking out of his hand.

Did Xander just stab him with a fork?

"Don't ever touch what's mine. Because the next time you do, I'll be taking one of your fingers with me."

I watch in horror as Xander pulls the fork from Benny's hand. Benny clutches it to his chest, "Of course, my apologies. She's quite a delicacy... a temptation."

Xander clenches his jaw so hard I can see the muscles quiver. "Believe me, I know."

I glance over to Damon, who has Keira pulled into his side, his arm wrapped around her protectively. She looks just as shocked and disgusted as I do. Damon, on the other hand, smirks as if he's just heard a good joke. I can't imagine how any of this could be considered funny.

"I look forward to seeing you all again soon." Benny smiles and walks out of the room. My eyes move to the bloody tablecloth.

"Well, my appetite is ruined," Damon chuckles, his eyes trained on his brother. "I wasn't expecting dinner and a show, brother."

Xander shakes his head, a smile ghosting his lips. "He's a fucking creep and you know it." Confusion sinks into my bones. I don't understand why they're smiling at each other. Xander just stabbed someone in the hand. Shouldn't they be trying to hide the tablecloth?

The waitress walks in the room a moment later, fear visible in her eyes.

"We'll take the check, please." Xander doesn't even look at her when he speaks. She rustles through her things before pulling out a receipt. She hands it to Xander, her eyes moving to the tablecloth once more. She scurries away without another word, and we walk out front. Once again, I keep my eyes trained to the floor, and walk arm in arm with Xander, standing beside him as he pays the bill.

I lean into his side and whisper in his ear, making certain no one is nearby, "What about the tablecloth?"

He turns his head slightly and gives me a boyish grin. The smile makes him seem more boy next door than notorious mobster, "Are you afraid that someone might come after me?"

I chew on the inside of my cheek, shaking my head no.

At my response, he leans in closer, his breath fanning against my lips. He's so close I could kiss him if I really wanted to. Instead, I inhale his scent; sweet whiskey and cinnamon cloves tickle my nostrils. It's an intoxicating scent, and it warms my body all over.

"Don't worry, Mouse, nothing's going to happen to me. I left her a little extra to cover it, and I doubt with the tip I gave her she's going to be complaining."

"Okay," I whisper softly, pulling back.

Xander guides us out of the restaurant and the limo is once again waiting for us along the curb. There's a chill in the air, and it settles deep into my lungs with every breath I take.

"All right, Mouse, it's time to see if that sister of yours is alive," Xander whispers into my ear as we climb into the limo. I settle into my seat, my hands in my lap.

My response to Xander's comment dangles on the edge of my tongue. I want to tell him that she's strong. Naive, yes. Young, yes. But she's a fighter, and she'll persevere through anything, even the darkness.

I never considered her not being alive, because that would mean this was a lost cause, but either way we weren't just here for my sister. Xander wanted to find his father. I'd known this since the moment I met him, and I'd bet anything his father had everything to do with my sister disappearing, so wherever my sister was, Xander's father wasn't far behind.

"I'm taking Keira back to the hotel. This has been far more than enough fun for her, I think." I peek up over at Damon through my lashes and notice Keira is in his arms and unusually quiet. She doesn't even look my way. In fact, her face seems to be burrowed into Damon's suit jacket. I'm going to guess she is also not used to seeing people get stabbed with forks.

"We'll drop you off." Xander motions something to the driver and the limo starts moving.

We stop a few minutes later at the hotel where Damon and Keira get out. "Be careful, and call me if you need anything, and if you find him..." I catch the look in Damon's eyes. It promises murder, mayhem, and pure chaos.

"Of course, brother, we're a team. If I find him, it'll be with you." Xander's voice holds promise, and I realize that even though he doesn't truly show it, he loves his brother.

Damon closes the door a second later and as soon as we are alone in the limo, Xander pulls me into his lap. I cuddle into his chest, burying my face into the crook of his neck, inhaling his unique scent. It's crazy how safe I feel in his arms, knowing the same hands and body that makes me feel safe and pleasured are the same ones that kill and destroy people's lives.

"Do you always stab people with cutlery?" I whisper into his skin, my hands making their way underneath his suit jacket. I feel his muscles tighten beneath my hands and wonder when he gets the time to work out.

He sighs, his hand stroking my head. "Only the ones who try to touch you." His response makes me smile, and I place a kiss over his throbbing pulse. I'm positive I'm falling head over heels in love with him... and the scariest part isn't that he's a murderer, or that he's thinks he's a monster. The scariest part is that I know there isn't a damn thing that can stop me.

I'm in deep... falling into darkness, hoping to find his hand.

14

Xander

"Where is this auction at?" Mouse asks softly. With her small body in my lap, cuddled up to my chest, I can feel the warmth of her body clinging to mine. It makes me want to bend her over the seat and fuck her. But I know how important this is for her, being close to me, so I rein in my need, saving it for later tonight.

"It's at a high-end strip club a ways out of town. They have a basement with by-invite-only events. Tonight's auction is one of their most popular."

It's not long before we pull up to the large square building. It has no sign on it, making it look like an old abandoned warehouse to any unsuspecting outsider. But to men like me, it's a playground for the rich and powerful to buy and sell in the flesh.

"My sister might be in that building." Excitement shows in her features as she pulls away, gazing through the window. "I just want to run in there and call out her name, see if I can find her."

"I know, but you can't. We must remain as inconspicuous as possible."

Mouse shivers in my arms, and I know she can hear the warning in my voice.

"If you do anything... if you step out of line once... I'll have to do something that neither of us are going to like. There are worse people than me in this world and most of them are going to be in this room."

She moves off my lap and I let her, missing the warmth of her body as soon as it's gone. "I understand. I just want to find her. That's all. I won't do anything to draw attention to us."

Worry worms its way into my mind. Mouse is desperate to find her sister, and desperation makes you do things without thinking them through. I just hope like hell for the both of us that she can keep up the act even if she does see her sister. Because if she doesn't, I'll have to hurt her, and that's the last damn thing I want to do. The driver opens the door, and I give Mouse one last look before we exit the car.

She loops her arm into mine and we walk up to the front door together. A large metal door opens and a heavy-set guy in a suit appears in front of us. His face doesn't have a speck of emotion on it. I reach into my jacket and grab the paper invitations, handing them to him without a single word. He eyes them slowly and steps aside to let us in. I glance over at Mouse, who is behaving well so far, keeping her eyes on the ground. She half smiles at me when she sees I'm looking at her and her happiness sinks deep into my bones.

God, she has no idea how much I want her right now.

We walk down the long dark hallway, leading us to a wide stairwell. I slow my pace walking down the stairs because Mouse keeps tripping over her own feet. I have half a mind to toss her over my shoulder and carry her the rest of the way there, but that wouldn't be the kind of entrance we need. So, instead, I let her lean into me, and I walk slowly down each step.

When we get to the bottom of the stairs, I briefly stop and look around to take in the crowd. Smoke fills the air, stinging my lungs. My eyes move over the bar, and to the dozens of tables in front of a brightly lit stage. The lighting is dim, but I notice a couple familiar faces, none of which are on my shit list. I catch Mouse looking up curiously, her eyes wide and bright, most likely looking at every little nook to see if her sister is hiding. She takes in the sights and sounds, and I wish like hell that she didn't have to endure this, but life isn't fair and if we want to find her sister and, more importantly, my father, this is what we have to do.

I squeeze her hand tightly as a reminder to keep her eyes down, and she complies. I walk her to a table closest to the wall and sit her down in one of the chairs. I like to keep my back to the wall, so no one can sneak up behind me. When you have as many enemies as I do, you don't ever let your guard down.

A cocktail waitress in nothing but some panties and a bowtie walks up to the table, a bright smile on her red painted lips. I hear a slight gasp from Mouse, as I'm certain she noticed the waitress is topless. I order her a glass of wine and myself a whiskey. She could use a little something to take the edge off.

The waitress tramps off, and I shrug out of my jacket. The room is hot with all the bullshit these high society men are spewing. When the waitress comes back with our drinks, I see two of the guys I typically do business with walking our way. Mouse squeaks beside me, clasping the wine glass between her small hands.

"Xander Rossi..." I hear Blaine chuckle as I take my glass of whiskey into my hands and lean back in my chair. It's easy to fool people into believing you're relaxed when you've been doing it for years. Charlie, his partner, gives me a nod, his eyes closing in on Mouse, who is fidgeting with the wine glass now.

"Blaine. How are you?" I see the curiosity and desire pool in his gaze when he notices her sitting beside me. I usually don't have a woman with me when I come to these kinds of events. Matter of fact this might be the first time he's ever seen me accompanied by a woman.

"Good, very good actually. We're planning on setting up some new distribution. Your brother still selling, too?"

I swirl the whiskey around in my glass. "Of course. We're running a fucking empire, Blaine. You don't just stop whenever you want."

Blaine nods, his eyes still on Mouse. I'm growing slightly irritated with each passing second. Yes, she's beautiful and yes, she oozes a naivety most men would love to have but she is mine. All fucking mine, and I'm not sharing her with any of these fuckers.

"I figured, but word on the street is that he got married."

I nod, taking a drink from my glass. The burn of the whiskey down my throat heats my cold insides. "He did. But he's still fucking working for me. Why are you so interested in my brother's work? Afraid he's going to outsell you?" I smirk, watching as his cheeks heat.

"He fucking wishes he could."

"Lucky for us, drugs are always in high demand. It's not like junkies are going stop using tomorrow." I glare at Blane and the fucker is still eyeing Mouse. My annoyance turns into full-blown rage now.

My grip on the glass tightens. "Is there a reason you're fucking staring?"

"Of course, not... I was just wondering if maybe you'd consider selling her." For the second time in one night, I've been asked to sell Mouse, and it's starting to weigh on me. All this time I was worried about Mouse blowing our cover, when it might just be me.

"This one is not for sale," I grit out.

"She must have a tight as fuck pussy..." He pauses briefly, his eyes flickering with lust. I'm literally a millisecond away from pulling my gun out and putting a bullet in his head. Business partner or not, he's taking shit too far.

"How about I buy you a new one tonight and you let me have this one? I won't break her, too badly." He chuckles as if something he said was amusing.

I blink slowly. Did this fucker really just say what I think he did?

"How about you turn around and walk away before I put a bullet in your brain?"

Blaine laughs, thinking I made a joke. The funny thing is... I don't joke.

"Okay, I get it. Final offer, take it or leave it. You keep her but you let me join in for a night. Just like the good old days?" Mouse moves around in her seat as if she's uncomfortable, and when Blaine moves a hand toward her face, I almost growl.

"Come on, Xander… What's she got that makes you want to keep her? All the girls on that stage tonight are virgins. Surely, she can't be with you and be as pure as snow."

"It doesn't matter what she's fucking got. I said she's not for sale. That should be a good enough answer for you, shouldn't it?"

Blaine grips her by the chin, and Mouse, unexpecting his touch, flinches away. Her movements cause the glass of wine to tip over, spilling across the front of her dress.

Fucking Christ.

"Whoops… I guess you have to take it off now," Blaine says, winking at Mouse. "Let me know if you need helped out of that dress. I'm pretty good with my hands, and even better with my cock."

She blinks, her long lashes fanning against her cheeks as she lifts her gaze to mine. I can see she's afraid. Afraid of the unknown, of what I'm going to do to her, or maybe she's worried I'll let this bastard have a taste of her.

But that's just it; she doesn't have a fucking thing to worry about. No, because my sweet mouse belongs to me and only me.

"Go get cleaned up in the bathroom," I order harshly. She shoves from the table, walking on unsteady legs. I worry she may fall flat on her face but the more steps she takes, the more she straightens out.

"Fuck, she has a nice ass." I look up to find Blaine staring in Mouse's direction. "I'm sure it's real tight, too."

My face deadpans, and I'm no longer able to allow him to make comments about Mouse. My blood reaches its boiling point with his last comment, and I can't stop myself from lashing out. I stand up and step into his personal space, our faces only a few inches apart. He loses his smirk immediately and his body visibly stiffens. Charlie actually takes a step back.

"If you don't fuck off right fucking now, I will break your neck where you stand. Do you hear me?" I don't want to cause any more of a scene, so I keep my voice low. It might be dumb of me to fucking take up for Mouse. I know it's dumb of me, but I won't let anyone hurt her. The only fucking bastard who gets to taint her soul is me.

"All right, Xander." Blaine takes another step back, his hands in the air as if he means no harm. Lying piece of shit. He turns around, taking Charlie with him, and I settle back into my seat, knowing this is going to put a target on my back.

Fuck, Mouse, I hope you're worth it.

"Welcome, welcome, gentlemen..." The announcer's voice bellows through the speakers, and into my ears, and I realize then that Mouse still hasn't returned from the bathroom and that could mean one of two different things.

She either ran... or.... I can't even fathom the later, so I'm going to fucking pray she went looking for her sister, because if something happens to her, I will burn down this entire fucking city.

15

*E*lla

I DON'T LIKE BEING HERE. Not even one bit, and I cannot imagine what my sister is going through right now, if she is even here. I scrub the front of my dress with a wet paper towel, but it doesn't do any good. It just makes the stain appear darker. I shiver, thinking of the way that Blaine guy looked at me. I dab harder at the soft material. He asked Xander to share me, insisting that they'd done that before.

Will he share me? With him... or with someone else? I gaze at my reflection in the mirror. Am I good enough to keep Xander's attention? I don't really know. I'm not nearly as attractive as some of the other women here, and god knows, I'm not even close to being as experienced.

My chest aches at the thought of being tossed aside like garbage by him. He's all I have right now. He saved me and losing him would kill me. I know it. With one fleeting look at my disheveled reflection, I shake my head. I move toward the door, feeling more down about myself now than I did before I came in.

At least Xander didn't get mad at me for spilling the wine, so that's a win, I suppose. I toss the wet paper towel into the trash and head out the door. I know I should keep my gaze to the floor, but I can't pass up the opportunity to check out my surroundings. I mean, I can't find my sister if I'm not looking for her. My gaze moves across the room, taking in each and every person.

I almost lower my head and place my eyes on the floor to walk back to the table when I pass a hallway. I stop dead in my tracks and peer down it. I'm not sure what compelled me to stop, but I did. My heart skips a beat and my throat tightens when I catch a glimpse of a set of big blue eyes almost identical to my own. *Violet.* It's only for a fraction of a second that I see her, but it's enough to get my legs moving.

I run down the hallway as fast as my feet will go, pushing someone out of the way without looking or apologizing. I don't care about anyone or anything. Just getting to my sister before it's too late.

"Vi!" I call out to her, trying to get her attention. I'm not far behind her, but I'm not close enough to stop the guy with a neck tattoo from dragging her toward the door in front of them.

She is half naked, wearing some type of lingerie... and I cringe seeing the bruising on the side of her face. She turns when she hears my voice but the guy dragging her just picks her up and carries her through the door.

She doesn't even struggle in his grasp, and I wonder if they've drugged her to make her comply. Her eyes are sad, and I'm angry, so damn angry. I'm almost to the door when someone grabs me from behind and slams me against the opposing wall face first.

The air is knocked from my lungs, and my face slides against the brick wall. I let out a whimper from the stinging pain of my flesh sliding across brick.

"Not so fucking strong when you're without that bastard, huh?" I struggle in the man's grasp, realizing I know that voice from somewhere. I open my mouth to tell him to get off of me when I feel a prick in my arm. In an instant, warmth coats my insides. My skin heats, and I start to feel woozy.

No, no, no, I am so close to getting Violet; this can't be happening. I struggle against his hold, but my strength is withering away by the second.

"If he wants you so badly, I guess he'll have to pay for you again."

I put the puzzle pieces together.

"Benny, what did you...?" The words come out slow, very slow. I'm turned around, coming face to face with my captor.

"Trust me, you don't want to go with Ivan, he is a crazy Russian. He'll just kill you without any of the fun." Benny smirks and pushes me toward another door.

I want to resist but my body and my brain are not on speaking terms right now. I can barely stand on my own, let alone make an attempt to run away or stop the asshole who has ahold of me.

My eyes droop, and I feel like I'm watching everything happen right before my eyes, yet there is nothing I can do.

Benny opens another door and shoves me inside. The motion sends me falling to the floor on my knees. I know I land harshly against the tile, but I feel no pain, nothing at all actually. There are people moving about in the room, minding their own business.

"Put her in the lineup," Benny orders, walking away from me like I'm a piece of trash. I open my mouth to scream at him, but my tongue feels impossibly heavy. I slap a hand against the floor to get his attention, but he doesn't even turn around. Instead, another man grabs me. His touch is rough, almost bruising, as he rips my dress from my body, leaving me in nothing more than my red thong and matching bra.

I know I should be screaming by now, but I can't bring myself to actually do so. I shiver, feeling the need to wrap my arms around my midsection and cover myself.

"Beautiful," I hear someone whisper into the hollow of my ear.

There are other women in this same room. My eyes glaze over each of them as they push us all into a single formed line. No one fights or cries. They merely conform just as I am.

"All right, ladies, let's make some big money tonight," someone hollers off to the right. I hear loud, booming voices, but I'm not sure what is going on. My knees buckle, and I sway unsteadily on my feet.

I have to lean against the wall behind me to keep myself from falling again. I close my eyes for a moment, trying to clear my head but that just makes it worse. A few moments later, the guy who took my dress off is back. I try and move away from him, but my legs won't work.

What is wrong with me?

With his hand on my arm, he makes me walk to a curtain. I see lights off in the distance. They're blinding, and I shake my head, wanting to tell them man no.

"All you've got to do is walk out there and stand next to the auctioneer. Got it, sugar?"

Without waiting for my answer, he pulls the curtain to the side and gives me a nudge. My chest heaves, and my body tingles as I barely make it across the stage. I can feel my body swaying like a leaf in the summer breeze.

When I make it to the center of the stage, I peer out onto the crowd. Men. All men. Their eyes took in every single inch of my flesh. The stage light is directly in my eyes, making it hard to see farther than the first row but that is all it takes to make bile rise up in my throat. I squint my eyes, attempting to look farther out onto the crowd. I can feel tears in my eyes.

Xander. His name goes off inside my head like a fire alarm. He'll save me, right?

"This lady in red is a very special treat. I bet you she tastes as good as she looks." The man chuckles, his eyes gleaming with lust. "We'll start the bidding at one hundred thousand."

"Five hundred thousand," a man's voice bellows through the room. A voice that is not Xander's. Panic fills my belly. Inside, I'm scared to death, but on the outside, I'm numb, completely numb.

"One million." A deeper, darker voice fills the room. *Xander.* My knight. My dark as sin hero. I want to run to him but when I take a step forward, the auctioneer grabs onto my arm, keeping me in place.

"One point five million." The crowd has turned completely silent, all chatter ceases at the bidding war Xander and this other guy have.

"Two million." I can feel the anger in his words. Is he really going to spend two million dollars for me? The amount seems utterly ridiculous. I couldn't dream of ever having such a large sum at my disposal.

"Do I have two point five million?" the auctioneer prods.

"Why the hell not? Let's go with three million." The unknown man's laughter fills the room.

"Five million," Xander counters not even a second later. There is no hesitation to his voice, and though he might be paying for my body, I know it will actually be me paying him later on.

"Six million, anyone?" the auctioneers prods once more, and the entire room remains silent. "Going once..."

My stomach clenches into a tight knot.

"Going twice..."

I can feel Xander's eyes on me even though I can't see him.

"Sold. For five million dollars to the man at table six."

The auctioneer ushers me to the other side of the stage, where yet another man is waiting for me. He grabs me by the elbow and walks me down a single flight of stairs. My legs feel like rubber, and my head is spinning. I feel sick to my stomach, and I wonder what's going to happen next? I screwed up with my sister, and now Xander's going to hate me for making a scene, the one thing I wasn't supposed to do.

"Five million, that's a pretty penny. We don't have many girls who bring that kind of money."

He leads me into another room that holds nothing but a chair. He pushes me down into it, my pantie-covered bottom slamming into the cold metal. The room is mostly dark, minus a small overhead light. I can barely make out the man's dark features.

"As soon as your buyer pays, he'll come back here and pick you up." He turns and heads back out the door, leaving me sitting there as if I'm waiting for the bus or something. The door shuts and the click of the lock being turned fills the room.

I feel afraid again, my emotions heightened by ten. Tears fall from my eyes, sliding down my cheeks. I can't lift my hands to wipe them away though. Nothing on my body wants to work.

I feel like such a failure... I couldn't save my sister. She was right there, and I couldn't get to her. Now she is gone again, and it's all my fault. How am I going to find her now? Xander will never help me again after what's happened tonight.

Time seems to pass slowly, and I don't know how long I've been sitting here crying my eyes out, wallowing in my own misery, until I hear voices in front of the door. The lock turns, and the door pushes open. Light streams into the room, hurting my eyes.

I avert my eyes to the floor. I don't have to look up to know who it is that walked in. Seconds later, I feel something being draped over my body before two strong arms wrap around me and lift me up.

I slam my eyes shut as Xander walks me out of there. I don't want to see anyone looking at me, and I'm not ready to see the anger in Xander's eyes. Instead, I lean my head against his shoulder and concentrate on his unique scent. Everything spins around me, and I know I need to tell Xander who did this before I end up passing out. I look up at his face. He's so handsome... like an angel who lost his wings. A dark angel.

"Be... Bennn..." My voice is so small he can't understand me, but he knows I'm trying to say something. I can tell from the wrinkle in his forehead.

He leans into my face. "How did this happen, Mouse? Tell me, and I'll kill them right now. Who did this to you?"

Warm tears cascade down my cheeks, "Benn...neee..." I focus all my energy into each syllable. I know the moment Xander realizes what I'm saying because his dark eyes fill with murder. The darkness lingers, and I wonder how deep it truly goes.

"Benny?" he questions softly, and I use all my remaining strength to nod my head.

I feel myself fading fast, my body softening in his arms.

"Sorry." The word comes out messy, but I hope he understands them and understands how sorry I really am. I screwed it all up and made him spend a crap ton of money.

"You were worth every penny, Mouse," he murmurs into my hair, and my eyes close one last time, the sound of his heartbeat lulling me off into the darkness.

~

I BLINK my eyes open very slowly, trying to make sense of where I am and what happened. My mind feels like it went through a blender. The room is dark, but the door is open and light filters in through the slit in the door.

I press my hands down and realize I'm in a bed, but I don't know the room I'm in. I jerk into a sitting position and the room spins around me like I'm on a never-ending carousel ride. I groan, holding a hand to my head, but the noise makes the continual pounding harder.

The shadow of a large figure appears in the doorway.

"How are you feeling?" Damon's thick voice fills the room.

Why is Damon here? Confused, I try to make sense of all the jumbled thoughts running rampant in my mind.

My gaze drops down to my body, and I notice that I'm wearing nothing but a bra and a thong under Xander's suit jacket that is wrapped around me.

I blink and pull the jacket around me tightly, realizing that Damon has just seen me in my underwear.

"Let's not tell Xander about that," he chuckles. I don't smile. In fact, I feel like puking. My emotions are unhinged, and I know something bad happened.

"What happened?" My voice cracks, my throat throbbing.

"You don't remember?"

I squeeze my lids shut for a moment of peace to try and comprehend all that took place, but my brain won't shut up.

"Not everything," I admit.

"That's okay. You were injected with some drugs, so memory loss is going to be pretty common. You should start to remember everything soon, just give it some time."

"Where is Xander?" From the fragments of memories that swirl in my mind, he must be furious with me.

"He'll be back soon. Hold on. I'll get you some water." Damon disappears and returns with a glass of water moments later. I take it from his hand and take a greedy sip. The cool water soothes my dry and scratchy throat.

A picture of my sister's face enters my mind.

"She was there..." A low sob escapes my throat. "My sister... she was there. Someone took her right before the auction. I saw it happen when I get out of the bathroom. She was right there... but I couldn't get to her and then..." I pause, pulling another piece to the puzzle from my memory. "And, Benny... Oh, god, he took me and gave me to those men and..." I cover my mouth in horror.

"And then Xander paid five million dollars for me." My heart cracks wide open, tears fall, and I couldn't stop them even if I tried.

"Hey... it's okay." Damon's voice sounds soothing but he's not the man I want to soothe me.

Hell, I'm not even sure if I should be telling Damon any of this. I don't even know if I'm supposed to talk to him at all. It probably doesn't matter, Xander will hate me anyway.

"It's not okay." I ball my hands into fists, slamming them down on the soft mattress beneath me. "I betrayed your brother's trust. I didn't save my sister. Xander is going to hate me. Everything was for nothing. Can't you see that?" I scream.

"It wasn't for nothing. At least you know that your sister is alive. And Xander doesn't hate you. No way in hell would my brother pay five million dollars for something he doesn't care about." Damon enters the bedroom. "And there is no one he has ever killed for except me... and now you. So, if you think hate is the emotion my brother feels for you, you're sorely mistaken."

I shake my head, refusing to believe him. "Trust means everything to him. I went down that hallway instead of coming to get him." I'm a blubbering mess, spilling all my secrets to some man I don't even know. "I chose to save my sister over going back to him."

Damon's face remains impassive. "Yeah, and family does that for family. You love your sister, and it shows. Look at all you've sacrificed to find her."

"Well, it means nothing now. I don't even know where she is or who took her." I swipe at some tears sliding down my cheeks. My face hurts. In fact, my entire body hurts.

"We'll find her again. Don't worry about that now." As silence blankets us for a moment, I realize I've just had a whole conversation with Xander's brother, a man who is his complete opposite in every way. And I know in the big scheme of things there are more important things to worry about, but I have to ask the question burning at the tip of my tongue. "Why are you and Xander so different?"

Damon gives me a little sideways smile. He looks so much like his brother, they could be twins if there wasn't an obvious age gap between them.

"I'm starting to think we are not all that different after all."

"What do you mean? You're married, happy, and have a baby coming soon. Your brother... he doesn't seem to want happiness."

"Everybody wants happiness, Ella. But Xander doesn't think he can have it. He doesn't think he's worthy." Damon pauses, and he seems lost in thought for a moment before continuing, "He has this irrational fear that anyone who loves him is in great danger... which is not that far off. He does have some enemies who could come after you. Being with my brother puts a target on your back. But loving the person you want to spend the rest of your life with, waking up every day next to them, it makes it worth it."

There's so much honesty to his words it seems like he's speaking from experience. I tug Xander's jacket around my midsection, wanting to feel warm.

I don't know why I ask Damon the next question I do, maybe I'm curious, or hopeless? Or maybe I'm a gunning for punishment. "Do you think your brother loves me?"

"Whatever he is feeling for you… it's pretty damn close to it." I want to ask him more, sensing that this is a rare opportunity to have Damon on the spot like this but before I can get my next question out, we are interrupted by the sound of the front door opening.

"Stay on the bed," Damon orders and walks out the door. I hear him saying something off in the distance, but I can't make out what.

Then I hear Xander's voice and damn near sigh in relief. *He is here.* I want to jump up and run to him but decide it's probably better to wait here for him.

A moment later, I hear the front door open and close again. Did he leave? I can hear my pulse in my ears. My eyes never waver from the bedroom door and when Xander's tall frame shadows the threshold, my heart stops beating for a few seconds.

My eyes rake over his body. He is wearing everything he was when we went to dinner, though his clothing is ruffled up like he slept in it, but that's not what really catches my eye. No, it's the blood stains splattered across his shirt that get my attention. Then I see his hands, which are almost completely red. As if he dipped them in red paint and pulled them out.

"Are you hurt?" My lips tremble as I ask. I'm not sure what I'd do if he was hurt because of my stupid actions.

"It's not my blood, Mouse." He simply answers, no real emotion to his voice. He starts unbuttoning his shirt and walks into the bathroom. I hear him turn on the shower, but I remain on the bed. He didn't ask me to come with him, and I'm not sure what kind of mood he is in right now. Plus, I've done enough disobeying tonight.

16

Xander

I watch the blood swirl down the drain. I killed again for her. I killed Benny, and I didn't care one fucking bit. Hell, I wish I could bring him back to life and kill him again just for doing what he did to her.

I want to be mad at her... I want to fucking hurt her, but she didn't do anything wrong. She didn't ask to be put up on that stage or drugged. My sweet, innocent mouse didn't ask for any of this. She just wanted to find her sister, and she ended up getting me instead.

I try and push the memory of her standing on that stage all alone from my mind, but I can't shake it. I can't shake how close to losing her I was. That bastard would've never outbid me, but that's not what fucking matters.

There was a chance I could've lost her, and that's like a fucking kick to the nut sack. I run my fingers through my hair, letting water cascade down my face. The plan was not to draw attention, and we all but took the spotlight and put it on us. There was no way that we were leaving with my father in our grasp now, no way in fucking hell. I want to punch my fist through the fucking wall. I'm so angry... mainly at myself. For putting Mouse in the situation I did.

I rinse once more before I step out and dry myself off. My eyes catch on the two bathrobes hanging next to the shower. A thought enters my mind. I might not be able to hurt Mouse, but I can regain control over her and that will calm the storm inside me, which is almost as good.

I slide the belts out of the bathrobes one by one and walk back into the bedroom. I know I'm a sick bastard, but I don't fucking care. My cock hardens at the sight of her. Her pouty lips are frowning. She is sitting on the bed still wrapped up in my suit jacket. She looks up at me with her big blues, full of fear and guilt.

"Xander, I..." I can see the guilt wash over her. She blames herself but she has no fucking clue how wrong she is. Tonight changed something inside me. It gave me a taste of what it would be like to lose her, and that's something I never want to go through again.

I hold up my now-clean hand to stop her from talking. "Not now, Mouse. No talking, we can do that later. What I need you to do right now is take off everything you are wearing. Toss it to the floor. Then crawl back up onto the bed."

Her eyes go wide, and she hesitates for a moment before shrugging off my jacket and undoing her bra. I watch her undo the clasps with shaking hands. By the time she gets her thong off, my cock is so fucking hard it hurts.

God, how did I get the most beautiful fucking woman to grace the earth?

I stand at the edge of the bed with the soft belts heavy in my hands. "Come here."

She timidly scoots over to me, barely meeting my eyes. Grabbing her chin gently, I tilt her face up, so she has no choice but to look at me.

"I'm not going to hurt you, but I need something from you. I need you to give up all control. I'm so close to the edge, Mouse, that I need this from you."

She blinks up at me as if she is trying to understand what I'm saying.

"Turn around," I order, when she doesn't respond.

She follows my command with less hesitation, now that I told her I wasn't going to hurt her. I take her arms and pull them backward so they meet in the middle of her back, her forearms kissing each other. I start looping one of the belts around her forearms then wrapping the ends around the middle. Once done, I tighten them together.

I hold onto her arms and lower her face first onto the mattress. She turns her face, her cheek resting against the sheets.

"You have no idea how much it killed me to see you on that stage tonight." I speak more to myself then her, watching as her tiny body shakes with unknown anticipation.

"I'm... I'm..." she starts to say, but I land a hard slap against her smooth ass cheek, cutting off her words. I massage the pink spot with my hand and lean over her body, my mouth finding her ear.

"Shhh, Mouse. You don't apologize tonight. Tonight, you take the pleasure I give you. You let me show you how crazy you fucking make me. You let me own you, the way you already own me."

I pull away and straighten back up. I drag my eyes down her body and trail a finger down her leg all the way to her ankles. I want her at my complete mercy, her body open to every inch of my swollen cock.

Taking the other belt, I loop it around her ankles.

"I'm scared, Xander." Her voice is shaky, her body trembling softly. I realize then that this is how my father tied her up. But the difference is that I want to give her pleasure, not pain.

"Don't be scared, Mouse. I'm not my father. I won't hurt you, never. Just trust me. Give yourself to me."

"Okay." Her small voice enters my ears and shoots right down into my soul. I promise myself that I won't lose control. I won't hurt my little mouse, never again, and neither will anyone else.

When I finish tightening the restraints on her ankles, I pull her body down to the edge of the bed and roll her onto her side. I push her knees up to her chest, so her ass and pussy are exposed to me.

I lick my lips when I see her pink slit all but begging for my cock. Using two fingers, I run them down the inside of her silky smooth thigh slowly, savoring every inch of her flesh. She's so soft, so perfect, so mine.

When I reach her center, I use those fingers to circle her already heated clit before I run them up and down her moistened slit. I can feel her growing wetter with each gentle stroke. Her breaths turn into heated pants, soft whimpers filling the room every time I move over her clit.

"Your body's reaction to my touch is unlike anything I've experienced before. Your body wants me without thought. It senses me; it knows the pleasure that only I can give you. Doesn't it, Mouse?"

I dip one finger inside of her when her wetness starts to coat it, and I know she is ready. I move my finger inside her very slowly, very gently stopping once I'm knuckle deep. She is still so fucking tight, her pussy squeezing my fingers just like she squeezed my cock nearly twenty-four hours ago.

I give her a moment to adjust and then I start moving in and out of her. I set a small rhythm and when my strokes become faster and her breathing turns into hard pants, I add a second finger.

"Come for me, Mouse." I plunge deeper inside her, bending my fingers slightly, to rub at that perfect spot at the very top of her pussy.

"Xander..." she gasps. "It feels... soooo..."

"I know, baby. I know. Come on my fingers. Show me how much you want this. How much your perfect pussy wants my cock."

Maybe it's my dirty words or just my deep precise strokes. I don't know but I feel the distinct flutter of her pussy muscles before she starts squeezing me so tightly it feels like she's trying to push me out. I pull my fingers out of her and roll her over onto her belly, pushing her knees upward.

She whimpers softly into the bed sheets as I move her, and I dip down between her legs, licking her slick pussy. Her sweet cream coats my tongue, the flavor exploding inside my mouth. My cock throbs, hanging heavily between us.

"Xander," Mouse calls out for me. Like a lighthouse against the shore, she beckons me forward, guiding me out of the darkness.

Fisting my cock in my hands, I move so that I'm directly behind her, the velvety smooth head of my cock probing her tight entrance.

"I'm going to fuck you hard, Mouse, so hard the air will still deep inside your lungs. So hard you'll feel me deep inside you every time you move."

"Please," she begs, and that one single word snaps something deep inside of me. I smirk, flexing my hips forward, plunging deep inside her. I listen as her breath hitches as I fill her to the hilt. I grip onto her hips with bruising force and slide all the way out of her, watching as her perfect pussy swallows my cock whole, taking every greedy inch I give it.

Gritting my teeth, I keep up the movements, in, out, in, out. Each stroke sends a shiver of pleasure up my spine. She's so soft, so fucking responsive, and so mine. Fuck, she's mine. All fucking mine.

"You belong to me, Mouse," I snarl, feeling all the blood in my body pump to my cock. I slam into her, again and again, feeling her pussy tighten around me.

"Yes." She pants into the sheets, her fingers reaching for me, but I don't want her touch. I want more, something deeper.

Without thought, I sink my fingers into her hair and force her head backward to look into my eyes while continuing to enter her hard. The sounds of our harsh breathing, and slaps of our bodies meeting each other echoes throughout the room.

"Fuck, Mouse, fuck..." I can't stop the words from escaping my mouth. Pleasure fills her eyes, and her body shakes slightly, her pussy squeezing around my cock as she falls apart.

An incoherent moan fills her throat, and I release my hold on her hair, shoving her face back down into the mattress.

She cries out, in pleasure or pain, I'm not really sure, but I'm too far gone to stop. I hold her in place, fucking her straight through her orgasm, forcing her to take more of me, deeper.

A tightening in my balls tells me I'm close, and I can feel Mouse's release dripping down over my cock.

"Mine. All fucking mine," I roar, slamming into her, my pace relentless, as an earth-shattering orgasm tightens deep inside me. The knot of pleasure unravels, and I explode, my sticky cum filling her tight womb. I hold myself in place, letting her tightness milk every last fucking drop of my release. My chest heaves, and my heart races. I've never come so hard before.

Her pussy quivers around my cock, pushing out our combined juices. My gaze drops down to where we were connected. I made her perfect pussy all messy.

I untie her arms, and then her ankles, watching as she sags to the mattress in exhaustion. I brush a few sweat-slicked strands from her face, lying down beside her. Her big blue eyes peer into mine, her cheeks are pink, and her body is thoroughly worked over. She looks like she might fall asleep, and I couldn't blame her if she did.

"I'm sorry for everything that happened tonight."

"No. You have no reason to be sorry. None at all. You did everything I asked you to do. But like I told you, there are worse fucking men than me in this world and you met them tonight."

"I found her," she announces, placing a hand beneath her cheek, like a small child would, as she continues to gaze at me. "I walked down that hall instead of coming back for you." Tears glisten in her eyes, and I know she feels guilty for doing what she did. But wouldn't I have done the same? Hadn't I? I'd killed or thought I killed our father for Damon.

"I betrayed you... I put myself in a situation and got caught. I made you spend all that money on me. Money that I'm not worth." Guilt coats every word she says, and her bottom lip trembles. Her voice cracks me straight down the middle. She's beating herself up over something that has already happened.

"I already know, Mouse. I know everything. I killed Benny, but not without getting all the information I could out of him first." I felt no remorse over killing him either. He deserved to die."

"You... you aren't mad? You don't want to punish me? Or kill me?" I blink, realizing I need to let her know how important she is to me. Maybe paying five million dollars to save her and have her as my own wasn't enough. Maybe I need to tell her... with my voice

"No, Mouse. I don't want to hurt you, and I won't, nor will anyone else. You belong to me, and I..." My voice trembles. "I belong to you." I whisper into her hair, pulling her into my chest.

"You... you love me?" She sounds shocked, as if she can't believe what she is hearing.

I chuckle. "I don't know if I can ever love anyone, but I care about you, and I think that's the same thing. I've killed for you. I've protected you. I've showed you kindness that I don't even show my brother... so if that's what love is, then yes... Yes, I love you."

"Xander." My name falls from her lips on a sigh and I know I'll never get tired of hearing her say it. I'll never get tired of having her as mine, because for once in my life, it feels like I've found a home.

"Mine," I growl, holding her tighter.

Always mine. Always.

17

*E*lla

WHEN WE RETURN HOME from Vegas, Xander and I get into a normal routine, or as normal as being with a criminal can be. I start to feel less like a prisoner and more like a member of his family. He treats me with the same respect he gives his brother and even leaves me with his son here and there.

I start to get comfortable with the idea of being his and maybe us being together but there are so many unknowns to our situation.

Xander comes with a heavy price tag... one that could cost me my life, and after Vegas, I'm not certain I'm prepared to go against any of his future enemies. I eye the adorable little boy sitting on the floor in front of me.

He just hit the six-month mark the nanny told me when I came in to feed him this morning. He was trying to bend upward like he wanted to sit up, so I put him on the floor and surrounded him by five pillows in case he falls over. Now he's giving me a slobbery toothless grin, and I can't help but smile back at him. He's adorable, looking like a complete miniature version of his father. He would be worth staying and being with Xander for, but the fear of never finding my sister again or dying at the hands of Xander's enemies is real and I can't shake the thoughts from entering my mind.

"You're just as handsome as your father," I coo at Q. His dark eyes sparkle with happiness, as he flings his chubby hands around. I think about all that Xander has done to protect his son, what he will continue to do.

"You think I'm handsome?" Xander's deep honeyed voice startles me and I jump, turning and craning my neck toward the door. I take in his devilishly handsome features. His black hair is slicked back, and his eyes look more brown then black today.

"It's not polite to eavesdrop." I smile.

"You and I both know that politeness isn't one of my strong points." He snickers and walks into the room. Immediately, he has Q's full attention and gives him a breathtaking smile. The love he has for his son shines through in everything he does and Q starts giggling and cooing while reaching for his daddy, opening and closing his tiny little hands.

"I'll be leaving soon."

"What do you mean, you'll be leaving soon?" I inquire.

Xander's eyes remain on his son. "I'm leaving, Mouse. That's all you need to know." My teeth grind together in anger. So, now we are back to this again, him not telling me what is going on.

"What do you mean that's all I need to know?" I shove up from my spot on the floor, coming to stand directly in front of him. The nanny walks in a second later, her eyes wide hearing our raised voices.

I didn't want to argue in front of Q, and I assume Xander doesn't either when he grabs me by the arm and pulls me in the direction of his bedroom.

"I do not appreciate your attitude, or the fact that you raised your voice in front of my son."

Rolling my eyes, I respond, "Well, I don't appreciate you not telling me what the hell is going on, so I suppose we're even then, right?"

Xander's grip on me tightens, his gaze blazing with fire. "You're rather mouthy, Mouse. Maybe I need to cuff you back to the bed and put something in your mouth to make better use of it."

Fear and arousal snake up my spine. "I... I don't mean to be rude, but I thought we were past keeping secrets. I thought you trusted me." My gaze falls to the floor, and my lungs deflate. I was so hopeful that Xander would help me find my sister, hopeful that he'd treat as more than just another girl, and maybe that was the problem with all of this. I was hoping for things that would never come true.

Xander's gaze drops to his hand on my arm and he releases me, taking that same hand and running it through his hair in frustration, ruining the perfectly slicked-back hair.

"I... I..." He stumbles over his words, his jaw clenched. "I'm going to meet with someone who knows where your sister is now. Benny gave me some information before I killed him. Damon found this guy a few days ago, and I set up a meeting with him. I'm hoping I can get the info on my father and find out where your sister is all in one go, but I didn't want to tell you because then you'd want to go."

"Of course, I'd want to go," I all but yell.

"And that's the fucking problem, Mouse. I can't have you going. Last time we were in Vegas, shit went down that shouldn't have." He leans in real close, his fingers ghosting against my cheek. I want to lean into his touch, but he pulls away before I get the chance.

"I can't risk losing you again. We came much too close last time, and I refuse to put you in danger again."

"I appreciate your concern, Xander, but it's my sister we're talking about." I'm determined to find her, to rescue her from the web she's gotten herself tangled in.

Xander smirked. "And that's precisely why you will not be going. You cannot think clearly when you put emotions into a situation such as the one we're in."

I want to stomp my foot on the floor, to beg and plead with him to go but it would do me no good. The look in his eyes tells me he isn't going to budge on his choice, and I don't particularly find the idea of being cuffed to his bed the entire time he is gone very exciting.

"Fine. But if you find her, can you at least have her call me? I just want to talk to her and make sure she is okay."

Relief fills Xander's features. "I will do my best. I cannot guarantee anything though, as I don't even know if the man I'm going to meet knows where your sister is. Benny could've been lying for all I know."

That was the truth; he could've been. But from what I remember that night, Benny had told me I didn't want to go with that man. I wonder if that man he called Ivan is the same person Xander is going to go and meet.

An image of my sister's face as she was carried through that door appears in my mind right then. Despair, sadness. She looked like she was exhausted and, once again, I was just a little too late. And just like our parents had let us down, I was letting her down.

"Everything is going to be okay, Mouse." Xander's gentle voice enters my mind and I blink back to reality.

"That's hard to believe when your sole purpose for living could possibly be dead." Tears well in my eyes, threatening to escape.

"She's not dead. That I can promise you. Will she wish she was dead when this entire ordeal ends? Maybe." Xander is so close now that I can't stop myself from leaning into his body, pressing my cheek to his chest, right over his erratic heartbeat.

"Do you think she'll hate me?" The tears finally started to fall, and when I feel Xander's huge hand against my back, holding me close, I release a ragged sob I wasn't even aware I was holding in.

"Shhh. After all you've done for her, how could she?"

I don't have an answer. All I know is that I let her down and the only way to make things right is to rescue her.

"I just want her to come home. I feel like I've let her down, and there isn't anything that I can do to make myself feel differently."

I wonder if Xander knows what it feels like to let someone down? He's always followed through on his actions, killing anyone he has to, to protect his family. Moments like this, I wish I could be more like Xander.

"I hate it, but I have to go." He pulls away from me, cupping me by my tear-stained cheeks, forcing me to look deep into his eyes. "I will do whatever I can to help your sister, and if I talk to her, I'll be sure to let her know you've been looking for her this whole time."

His words make me smile and warm my heart.

"Thank you," I whisper, right as his lips descend on mine. He kisses me with a longing for more, so much more. He has been kind to me, showing me what it is like to be made love to, while giving me just a shred of pleasure mixed in with pain. He held me every night, making certain I was secure, safe.

When he finally pulls away, we are both breathless, my lips are swollen from our kiss, and his eyes are glazed over with need.

"Watch over Q while I am gone, and don't even make an attempt to leave. I'll have my men posted at every exit of the house, and believe me, Mouse, if you do happen to get out, I will find you and make certain you never see your sister again."

I nod in understanding, knowing his words aren't only a warning but the truth. I'm not going to run though. Xander has too much hanging over my head. He is the only one who can help me secure my sister's safety and make sure she comes home.

"And when I get home, you're all mine. Every fucking delicious inch of you."

I gulp, his touch leaving me, making me feel cold all over. And with one last fleeting look, he's gone, leaving me alone, with a thousand different emotions swirling deep inside me. I stand in place with my feet cemented to the floor for a long time, long after I hear the front door slam closed.

And as soon as he's gone, I realize just how much I miss him.

I GRIP the edge of the toilet, the contents of my stomach emptying into the bowl for the third time in the last twenty-four hours. It's been a long time since I was sick enough to puke... years. My throat burns, and my eyes water as I try to hold back the illness from escaping my body. The muscles in my stomach tighten... and I grip the rim of the toilet harder. The bile in my stomach burns a path of fire out of my throat and into the toilet once more.

As I cling to the toilet, my eyes roam over the box of tampons that sits neatly on the back of it. My periods were all over the place, which made tracking them hard. I was on birth control for a while but hadn't been able to take my pills because of being held up in Xander's house. That, and well, I never considered to ask if I should go back on the pill. I guess that kind of led us to the situation we were in now.

With so many other things on my mind, the thought of birth control kind of went out the window. Xander never asked me, and I never mentioned it either. I couldn't actually remember the last time we used a condom, other than the first time we had sex.

"Shit," I mutter under my breath. Do I really need a pregnancy test to confirm being pregnant? Dread has coated my insides since last night. The last thing either of us need is a baby. I mean, Xander already has Q and that is hard enough for him.

And I don't even know if we could be considered a couple, since we've never really discussed that either. I sigh into the toilet before flushing it. It's obvious that I needed to sit down with Xander and figure out what the hell we are, and what we plan to do. I'm not his prisoner anymore, and he isn't my captor. We are beyond that now.

Thankfully, I'd already asked one of the maids to pick me up a pregnancy test yesterday. She'd told me she would bring it to work today, and the anxiety of the unknown is starting to wear on me.

Trying to calm myself, I wash my hands and brush my teeth before heading out of the bathroom. My eyes move to the clock beside the bed. It is nearly eight a.m., and she will be here any second. I want to get to her before anyone else can see what she is carrying. The last thing I need is a stupid rumor getting back to Xander before I can confirm or deny something.

Slipping into my flats, I head downstairs, trying to find her. I weave in and out of the halls heading toward the servants' quarters. When I don't see her anywhere, I turn around and head back toward the kitchen. I feel Xander's guards watching my every step, and I smile at one of the men, trying not to draw too much attention. He doesn't smile back, which doesn't surprise me. I get the feeling most of the men around here don't know what it feels like to smile.

When I spot Cara unloading bags of groceries near the pantry, I walk up to her, casually, of course.

"Did you get it?" I lean into her ear and whisper.

She smiles and pulls out a pregnancy test. I stare at the small box for a long moment as if the damn thing holds all the answers to my problems, and I guess it kind of does.

"Here you go, Mrs. Rossi."

I blink at the name. Doesn't she know? Maybe she just thinks we're married. I guess it doesn't really matter, but I'd feel weird correcting her and since doing so would just make her ask questions, I let her think whatever she wants.

"Thank you!" I exclaim, wrapping her up in a tight hug. Her body stiffens in my hold, clearly not anticipating my actions. "Seriously, Cara, it means a lot to me. If you need anything ever, please don't hesitate to ask." I could kiss her cheeks for helping me out with this, but I don't think she'd like that very much so instead, I release her and make my way back upstairs.

A couple guards pass me in the hall. They eye me warily but don't say anything or even greet me. They treat me like I'm not there, though the coldness in their stares makes me shiver. I wonder what Xander told them about me, and if they would attack me just like the other guard had.

No. They know better. I shake the thought away and continue onward toward the bedroom. Once inside, I open the box and take out one of the tests. It's wrapped up in a plastic packaging and crinkles loudly in my hands. I'm seconds away from taking the test when a noise just outside the door catches meets my ears.

I didn't see anybody else in the hall when I was out there a minute ago. Maybe the nanny is just going in to check on Q? I place the package on the dresser and peek around the corner and down the hall.

Deep in my belly, something feels off, and I think my body knows it, too, as I stay to the shadows, looking out the door. My eyes catch on an unknown man making his way down the hall. He's not dressed like any of Xander's men, and he's walking as if he is trying to be quiet. I try and think about who he might be, and where he came from.

His back is to me and with every step, he gets closer and closer to Q's bedroom. Whoever this man is, he shouldn't be here. None of the guards come up to the second floor. None. But I suppose I already know he's not a guard and that makes my suspicion of him that much more.

Xander's words echo inside my mind... *"Watch over Q."*

My instincts kick into overdrive. Whoever this bastard is, he isn't going to touch Q. Without thinking, I walk out into the hallway, tiptoeing behind the guy. Fear trickles down my spine but I push it aside. I need to make sure the baby is okay. *Protect the baby, above all else.*

He is already at Q's door, his hand on the knob, when I yell directly behind him, "Stop!"

He turns around, and I immediately regret that I hadn't thought this completely out. I should have grabbed a weapon or something because now I've got his attention but I'm standing in front of him completely helpless.

The look in the man's dark eyes promises death, and he lurches forward, trying to grab me. I scurry out of the way, feeling the air move around me as I do.

A scream builds in my throat, but before I can get it out, Q's bedroom door opens and one of the nannies appears in the doorway.

She takes one look at the man and starts screaming, "Someone help! Someone!" Her high-pitched voice makes my ears hurt.

The man smirks at me, a feral look that terrifies me. And then he springs into action. I cower in fear, afraid he may strike out at me or the nanny, but instead, he starts running down the hall right past me, while I still stand frozen in fear, my feet cemented to the floor.

I turn my head and watch him run toward the staircase. It seems strange that he would run straight toward the men that he knows will capture him... almost as if that's his intention. A guard appears at the top of the stairs, and then another, and then another. Within seconds, Xander's men are on top of the intruder and have him completely immobilized on the floor.

Only then am I able to suck in a shaky breath. I hold a hand to my chest, trying to calm my erratic heartbeat. I watch as one of Xander's top men, Aston, pulls out his phone.

What the hell just happened?

As soon as I get my bearings, I walk into Q's room, past the nanny who is crying hysterically against the door. I want to soothe her fears but the only person in this room that I care about right now is Xander's son. In a second, I'm at his crib, my eyes frantically moving over his body for injury. I know the man never got ahold of him, but the fact that he had every intention terrifies me.

I force myself to breathe normal, staring down at the dark-eyed cutie who is lying on his back, holding on to his own feet while rocking back and forth. He smiles widely when he sees me, completely unaware of everything that just happened around him.

I pick him up and take him into my shaky arms, cradling him against my chest. As soon as I feel his tiny heartbeat, I start crying. Xander's men enter the room, their eyes on me, studying me as I hold Q. They don't say anything, and then Aston appears in the doorway. He pockets the phone in his hand into his pants.

"Boss wants you and the baby to remain in his room until he gets home. I will be standing post outside the door." His words force me to start moving, and within a second, I am inside Xander's bedroom.

I'm not sure what it is that's got me in tears. Maybe it's the fear of someone hurting Q or maybe it's the fear of Xander losing the only thing that matters to him. I don't know, but all I know is that I won't be letting that baby out of sight until his father gets home.

Staring through tear-filled eyes down at the little boy in my arms, I vow to protect him, care for him, and never let the evil that's touched my life touch his.

18

Xander

THE AIR in my lungs freezes. I knew coming here was a bad idea. Even if I did find Ella's sister and strike a deal with Ivan, it isn't worth the risk of losing my son and the one woman making my heart beat for the first time since my mother. I'm on the plane and home in a few hours' time. The blood in my veins runs cold thinking of that fucking bastard touching my son or Mouse.

Thank fuck my men got him and tied him up in one of the interrogation rooms. I already know where my father is hiding, thanks to Ivan, but beating the fuck out of this bastard is exactly what I need. I'd teach him a lesson.

Plus, I still need to figure out how the fuck he got into the house without tripping any of the alarms or being seen by any of the guards. The thought of having another traitor in the house makes me want to kill everybody working for me, and I would if I didn't need the protection.

I down a glass of whiskey, hoping it will calm the nervous anxiety running rampant throughout my body. When it doesn't, I down another.

Fucking Christ, this is the longest fucking plane ride of my life. When we finally touch the ground, I all but run out to the car. I get in and tell the driver to floor it. I need to get to the fucking house right now before I go insane.

Every time I think about that guy touching what is mine, a little shred of my humanity fades away. After what seems like an eternity, we finally pull up to the house with squealing tires. I throw open the door before the car stops all the way and run up to the front door, slamming the door closed behind me. My feet pound across the floor, and I make my way through the house. I'm a man on a mission, and I don't give one fucking fuck what anyone has to say about it.

When I finally get to the second floor and gaze down the hallway, I find two guards standing in front of my bedroom door. They straighten up when they see me marching toward them, most likely afraid that I'll kill them.

"They're both in there, sir," one of them announces and opens the door for me, before taking a step back. I nod curtly and walk into the room, scanning it. When my eyes land on Mouse sitting on the bed holding Q in her arms, relief like I've never felt before washes over me slowly. My entire body seems to ease at the sight of them, and I slowly make my way to their sides.

Mouse's eyes fill with tears when she spots me. I take both of them into my arms, holding them close to my body. I breathe in Mouse's delicate female scent mixed with Q's pure baby smell, and I know I'm home.

"I'm so sorry. I should have been here." My fear of losing them is simmering now that I can see and hold them, but the anger inside me is just as strong as ever. One thought sticks out inside my mind over everything else now that I know Mouse and Q are safe.

Kill. Kill the bastard who tried to hurt your family...

"It's okay, we are okay now," Mouse whispers, trying to calm the storm beating against my insides. She has no idea how close to losing control I am. How much I want to kill, destroy, hurt...

"Good. I am glad you're both okay." I'm feeling conflicted. I want to stay here with Mouse and my son, but I know the job must get done. I cannot stand that this bastard is still alive. "I need to talk to this guy. I need to know how the fuck he got in here and then I need to kill him, send his head to whoever sent him our way."

Mouse shivers in my arms. I know I'm scaring her but I'm not going to lie to her about what I plan to do next. I plant a kiss on her forehead and one on the top of Q's head before I straighten and exit the room.

It's been a long time since I felt this kind of darkness creep in, and I'm afraid of what it might do to me if I unleash it completely. I have to remind myself that I'm doing this for them... to keep them safe... and to put out the flames of anger torching my insides.

∽

THE NEXT FEW hours go by in a blur. Blood covers my hands, and I've ripped my shirt off and thrown it to the ground. I've been working this guy over for I don't know how long now. I stopped thinking about how long I've been down here a while ago. The only thing that really matters to me is vengeance.

I stare down at the fucking piece of shit, wishing fire would come from my eyes. He's already admitted to knowing about Q and that my father is the one who sent him. He's told me that there was a traitor in my house, which is where my fears laid all along. Now I just need to get the name out of him, and I can kill that bastard, too. I won't rest until I've eliminated every single threat possible against my son and Mouse.

I will kill everybody who dares to get in my fucking way.

I crack my knuckles. There's so much blood... I worry he may die before I get the answers I seek out of him.

"I don't think you'll like the answer to the question you seek, Mr. Rossi."

I tilt my head sideways, examining his already bruised face. There is no way he is getting out of this alive, no fucking way, so I suppose I can offer him a quick death in return for his confession.

"Tell me who the fucking traitor is and I might kill you with a bullet to the head instead of leaving you to my men to finish off."

The guy doesn't seem to care about what I've said, and I can't contain my anger over his silence a second longer. Pulling my fist back, I uppercut him, sending him swaying backward on his chair. Then I cross the space between us and press my foot to his throat.

"I have no fucking patience for your games. I am not my father and I will fucking crush your windpipe without thought if you do not tell me what I want to fucking hear," I roar, pressing more firmly against his throat.

The fucker smiles through bloody teeth, a gurgle fills his throat, and I relish in the sound. I want to kill him so badly it's all I can see or feel, but I rein in the need, telling myself soon, so very soon. I pull away, letting air enter his lungs.

"Of course, you're not like your father," he wheezes. "He'd never let some girl run away with his heart."

I grind my teeth together. Of course, he knows about Mouse. He was sent here by my father.

"Tell me what you know," I grit out, pulling my gun from my holster.

The man's face darkens. "It is her. The girl you care for so much. The one who's run away with your heart. She is your traitor... she was our insider... she is the reason we know about your son. She is the one who opened the door for me so I could come inside without anyone knowing."

The world around me stops. Everything stands still. My heart cramps inside my chest. I can't breathe... I can't see. Everything around me darkens for a moment. I feel like I've fallen off the deep end and into dark stormy waters.

For I moment, I can't feel anything. I'm completely numb. This can't be real. He is lying. There is no way... A million images fill my mind, floating around my head like puzzle pieces I'm desperately trying to connect.

Could it be true? Could I have been so stupid, so careless? I did find her at my father's house... Is it possible she's been playing me this whole time? Waiting for me to let her inside my heart. The guards said they saw her downstairs just before... Why didn't she scream? My men told me they only heard the nanny scream for help. Mouse never called out for help. She never did anything...

I want to take the gun in my hands and place it to my own head. I want to shoot myself because hurting her will be just like hurting myself.

I shake my head. No, no, not Mouse...

The numbness starts to fade... Then, like a tidal wave, everything comes crashing into me at once. Betrayal, hurt, and an unbelievable anger. A deep fiery rage burns through my veins. It consumes every inch of me.

I place the barrel of my gun to the man's head and pull the trigger. His brains splatter across the wall and floor behind him, his eyes going vacant with death in an instant. I feel nothing... nothing at all.

I turn to Aston. "Go and get the girl. Bring her to me here." I squeeze my eyes closed, wishing this was nothing more than a nightmare. Wishing I didn't have to snuff the light out of her. Everything I've done in the last month was to protect her... to protect our future, and then she does this.

She betrays me just like the last woman in my life, Q's mother and my own mother the time before that... She's nothing. Nothing but a fucking hole for me to use and that's if I even want her by the time I get done with her.

I snarl, hearing her voice enter the corridor... she's fragile, so fucking breakable, and I'm going to enjoy breaking her... making her feel the same pain I do right at this very moment.

My little mouse has finally been caught in a trap... and this one she won't have anyone to help her escape from.

She steps into the room, her face white as a ghost. Her steps are timid and scared. Her hand comes up to her mouth as if she is trying not to puke taking in the scene presented to her.

"Xan—"

"Shut up!" I cut her off. She takes a step backward and looks up at me, her eyes impossibly wide. "I fucking trusted you... I fucking trusted you with my son. Everything I did the last month for you. I found your sister. Paid five million fucking dollars for you so that you wouldn't get raped and taken by some bastard, and the whole fucking time, you were playing me?"

She starts shaking her head as if she's going to say no but I'm already on her. My hand wraps around her small fragile throat. I feel her knees buckle, her body thrashing in my hold. I kick her feet out from underneath her and push her to the floor with my hand still at her throat.

I can tell she is trying to say something, but I won't listen to her. I don't want to hear her voice ever again. I squeeze harder until I know she is struggling for air. Tears roll down the side of her face, running down onto my hands. I feel small hands slapping at my bare chest, her tiny nails digging into the skin as she fights for another breath.

I should kill her right now... All I'd have to do is keep squeezing her delicate throat a little longer. Her creamy white cheeks are already turning a deathly blue, and her eyes are starting to drift closed. I know in my mind it won't take much more. Just a little bit longer and I'll never see her beautiful smile again, or the way she looks when she falls apart. Just a little longer and she won't be mine anymore, and I can rid my life of the stain she's left on my soul.

And yet I pull away, releasing her throat finger by finger, before shoving her to the unforgiving floor. I hear the slap of her skin against the concrete, but I don't care. I can't. She's betrayed me. She's made me weak.

I am weak. I can feel it.

I can't kill her. I can't fucking do it.

She takes in a sharp breath, filling her lungs. She wheezes as if she can't suck in enough air. Her hands clutch her chest, and she curls up on her side. I clench my fists, willing myself to point the gun at her and pull the trigger.

But I can't. I fucking can't and it kills me inside to know that I've let her get under my skin. That I've fallen in love with someone only for them to hurt me in the worst way. I stand there watching her as she lays on the cold floor, her eyes closed, sobs wracking her body.

"If I could fucking kill you, I would, but since I can't, I'll just make your life a living hell, taking from you every single thing you've taken from me. This time, I won't have mercy on you... not one fucking bit." Before she takes another breath, I'm walking out of the room.

"Take her to the cell," I order, before slamming my fist into the wall in front of me. The pain of the impact radiates up my arm. It hurts, but not as bad as the fucking muscle beating inside my chest.

Fuck love. Fuck life.

I walk up the stairs, forcing myself to keep going instead of turning around, because if I turn around and go back down the stairs, I'll end up killing her. Even though I'm angry, that would be my biggest mistake ever. I can get my revenge on her in other ways. Besides ending her life would be the easy way out.

I let the anger inside of me fester, and by the time I make it upstairs and into the bedroom, I'm ready to explode. This room, my bedroom that I fucking shared with her. I want it gone. I want everything gone.

It still smells like her. Her unique scent lingers, clinging to everything in here. I need to destroy everything that reminds me of her, everything of hers, everything she's touched or even looked at. I want to erase her from my life, from my fucking mind.

I start at the dresser, pulling out all the drawers and throwing them out in the hallway. Clearing out everything one by one. The nightstands, every last item of clothing in the closet. I throw it all out. I rip the sheets off the bed and flip the mattress over. It's not enough. I start kicking the dresser, over and over again until there is nothing left but a pile of fucking wood, but my anger is still uncontrollable.

With nothing left to destroy in this room, I start punching the wall. Bones crunch with every punch but I'm past the feeling of pain. Blood covers the wallpaper quickly. Leftover blood from the torture session is mingling with my own blood as I punch into the unforgiving wall until my arm gives out. I fall to my knees and let my face fall into my hands.

How did this fucking happen? How did I not see this?

I shake my head. Ransacking my mind for clues that I've missed. She never gave me a reason not to believe her. Everything she ever did seemed so fucking genuine. I lower my hands and look at them. They are swollen and covered in blood. I need a fucking shower, to rinse away the evidence of her betrayal. I force myself back on my feet and drag myself into the bathroom.

The light flickers on, and my eyes move over the bathroom. There are pieces of her littered throughout the bathroom as well. My eyes gloss over the counter, as I start to undo my belt, and that's when I see it.

There's a pregnancy test on the counter. I can't stop from walking over to inspect it. As soon as I'm in front of it, I see the distinct plus sign. Guilt and regret wash over me.

Mouse is pregnant... she's pregnant with my baby... *our* baby.

I race down the stairs, my heart beating so hard I'm sure it's going to burst out of my chest at any second. I run down another flight of stairs and then another, rushing into the basement. Whatever she's done is pushed into the back of my mind now that I know she is carrying my child. I can't leave her down here. I turn the corner and freeze. The cell door is wide open, and everything is empty.

My heart sinks into my stomach, and I feel like vomiting when I see the scrap of paper lying on the cot. She escaped. She fucking escaped.

I clutch the paper in my hands before opening it to read it. As soon as I do, every emotion inside of me evaporates into thin air.

A coldness sweeps through my veins...

Dearest Son,

It's *a shame that you couldn't be a better leader to our family name. Not only did you fall for every trick I put in front of you, you let another disgraceful whore into your home. I thought Damon was the stupid one, but you've been playing into my hand since I sent Q's mother your way to get pregnant. You played right into my hand without even thinking about the consequences and now I've come to claim what was originally mine to begin with. Thanks for breaking her in. I look forward to being the one to break her, since clearly you were too weak to.*

. . .

My entire body is shaking by the time I finish reading the letter... I pull out my cell and text Damon, telling him it's time. My one and only thought is to get Mouse back and kill the bastard for real this time.

19

*E*lla

THE GAG in my mouth stops my screams from being heard, but it doesn't stop me from doing everything I can to stop the miserable bastard holding onto me. I kick and thrash around as much as possible. My hands are bound behind my back. Cable ties dig into my newly healed skin. The monster's fat fingers dig painfully into my arm as he drags me behind him. The smell of dirt fills my nostrils as I kick it up in an attempt to slow him down. We're in some kind of underground tunnel in the basement... an escape entrance of some sort.

I try and tell myself that this can't be happening, but it is. Tears sting my eyes. I need to get away. I need to find a way to escape this man. I can't let him hurt me, not when I might be carrying Xander's baby. If anything, I need to fight for my unborn child.

With that thought, I dig my heels into the dirt in an attempt to slow him down.

It does nothing but make him grip me harder and grunt as he pulls me deeper into the tunnel. "Don't be difficult. The more trouble you give me, the worse I'm going to make it for you and believe me when I say I can make it very, very bad for you."

I shudder, trying once more to escape his dirty hands. "You have no idea how much fun I'm going to have breaking you. We're going to continue right where we left off." His words cause me to scream, and my throat throbs. What if Xander never comes for me? I recoil at the thought of becoming this man's whore. Of being used by him. It feels like my worst nightmares are becoming my reality. Bile burns up my throat. I can't vomit again, not right now. I take a deep breath, trying to calm myself.

He tugs on my arm again, and I almost fall over my own two feet.

"Let's go," he growls in annoyance without looking back at me. I wonder how he got onto the property, or even inside the house to get me without any of Xander's men knowing. My feet throb as we walk a few hundred more feet. Fresh cool air starts to fill my nose as we reach the tunnel's exit. Dirt underneath my shoes turns into wet forest ground as the night sky appears above us.

The evil man in front of me tugs me along, making me walk faster than possible with all the tree branches and thick brush. We walk another couple hundred feet until we come up to a car.

I pull back against his hold when he opens the trunk and turns to grab me. My effort is pointless. He smacks me with the back of his hand, sending me sailing to the ground. My cheek throbs, and an evil grin pulls at his lips.

"You're a real fucking bitch," he spits, before picking me up and tossing me inside. The trunk closes above me with a loud thud, leaving me in absolute darkness. The engine roars to life a few moments later, and the car starts moving, each bump in the road vibrating through me.

I thought I had been scared in the past, but nothing compares to the gut-wrenching terror consuming every part of my body. All my thoughts go back to Xander and how he looked at me. All the hate and hurt in his eyes. It felt like a knife twisting in my heart and now that's possibly going to be the last time I see him.

It can't be. I refuse to let it be the last memory we share. I have to live, because I have to protect our baby. But the more I think about it, the more I come up with nothing. There is no viable way for me to get out of this unscathed.

Xander is never going to come for me; I feel it deep in my bones. Not when he thinks I've betrayed him. Even if he were to try to find me, how long would it take him? How long would I able to endure his father's treatment without breaking? Even if I make it out of this alive...will I ever be the same?

I roll around in the trunk as Xander's father continues driving. I struggle against the cable ties that bind my hands. The next turn we take makes something wedge underneath me. I scoot around until I can get it into my hands.

It's cold and heavy, and made out of some kind of metal. I keep moving it around, my fingers putting an image of the item together in my head. A crowbar or something like it. I almost shout in victory. I try not get too excited about it though. It's not going to do me any good if I can't get my hands untied.

I move it so the sharp pointy edge is in between my hands. Then I wedge it right under where the cable tie is connected and push my body weight against it. It keeps sliding off instead of slicing through like I want it to, and I growl into the gag with frustration. My palms are sweaty, making it even harder to regain control every time it slips out of my hand.

Don't give up. Fight. I need to fight... fight with every single ounce of blood inside me. Xander might not come for me, but I have to try and escape this on my own. We make a right turn, which makes my body roll to the other side of the trunk. I right myself and we drive for a short time before the car comes to a complete stop. It's now or never.

I keep trying with all my strength to break the stupid cable ties, but they won't budge. Fear trickles down my spine when I hear the car door open and close. In that second, I decide to try one final time. I place the crowbar back into place and push as hard as I can. My heart's beating so fast, the pounding resonates into my ears.

The clicking sound of the trunk being opened fills the small space just as the cable tie snaps in two and my arms fall free. Moonlight pours into the space as the trunk opens. My stomach clenches as I curl my fingers around the cold metal of the crowbar and swing it at the face of the bastard who appears above me.

If I'm going to die, then I'm going to go out swinging. I hit the asshole in the side of the head, making him stumble backward.

"You fucking bitch," he snarls, clutching the side of his head. Before he has time to regain his bearings and reach for me, I climb out of the trunk, bringing the crowbar with me. I run as fast as my legs will carry me into the thick brush ahead. Vines, branches, and leaves stick to my clothes and scratch across my skin.

But I don't care. I don't look where I am going, I just run.

"Follow her. Don't let her get the fuck away." Xander's father's voice rings in my ears. I hear more voices behind me, and heavy footfalls snapping branches with every step I take, but I don't stop. I can't if I want to make it out of this alive. I remove the gag from my mouth and continue running.

Each breath that passes my lips is labored, and when I can't possibly take another step, I slip behind a tree, a shiver coursing through me as a cold breeze blows through the trees, rustling the leaves around me.

"Come out, come out, wherever you are..." An unknown voice calls out into the darkness. I force myself to breathe slowly, afraid that my breathing may give me away.

With the crowbar heavy in my hands, I prepare myself to use it. I hear men walking away from me and for a moment, I think there might be a chance they won't find me. My hopes are short lived when I hear a twig snap to my right, and a large figure cloaked in darkness appears at my side.

The urge to scream is strong but I know it will only give me away, so I swallow it down. I swing the crowbar in the air and hit the guy with all the strength I have left inside of me. My arms shake with the effort, and I end up hitting him in the shoulder instead of the head, where I was aiming.

He grunts and grabs the bar from my hands, pulling it out of my grip like it's nothing more than a piece of paper. I twist around and run the other way, but I only make it a few steps before another body slams into me, knocking the breath out of me and sending me to the wet ground. Rough hands grab onto my shoulders, holding me in place.

"Running is going to cost you extra, babe," the bastard whispers into my ear, and I grunt, trying to buck him off of me, but my weight is nothing compared to his. He presses his hardened dick into my backside, like this kind of thing turns him on or something.

"Let me go," I snarl, digging my fingers into the dirt for leverage.

"No can do," he mutters, his body moving off of mine. I attempt to make a run for it, but I don't even get up off the ground before he has his hands wrapped around my middle. He picks me up like I weigh nothing and throws me over his shoulder. Then he slaps a hard hand to my ass.

I grind my teeth together, holding back the yelp of pain.

"You should be glad you didn't hit my head with that thing. I would have been taking my turn before the boss got a chance."

"You'll never get a chance. Not if I kill you all." I pound my fists into his back, refusing to give up on escaping.

"Boss didn't tell me you were such a spit-fire." The man carrying me chuckles, continuing his walk back the way we had just come. "I really hope that he leaves you alive so I can play with you later. You'd make a great pet."

I grit my teeth in anger. I've never felt so much fury in my life.

The nameless man carries me all the way up to a house I had missed when I was running away. There are lights on inside that emit a small glow of light onto the outside porch. I look down, watching as the grass changes into patio stones beneath us.

"There she is." I want to throw up just hearing his voice.

"You didn't tell me she was such a feisty one, boss. I'd love to keep her as my pet." The man holding me lifts his hand, placing it on my ass cheek. I'm pretty sure I'm going to kill this bastard as soon as I get the chance.

"Let go of me," I seethe, pushing upward with my hands. The man's hand digs into my ass cheek, causing me to cry out in pain. A bubble of fear fills my mind. They are going to rape me, I know it. I can feel it, but I have to protect the baby above all else... I need to survive if only for him or her.

"You can have her when I'm done with her. That is if she survives what I have planned." Xander's father's voice cuts off my train of thought.

The sound of leaves rustling off in the distance has me lifting my gaze to the woods in front of me. I can't see worth a shit, but I know something is out there, lingering right on the edge of the clearing.

"Where do you want her?"

"I'll take her from here."

The man swings me off his shoulder and sets me on the ground. He pushes me forward, making me lose my balance and fall to my hands and knees.

The men all start laughing. "You better get used to that position, whore."

"Xander will come for me and kill you all," I lie. I'm not sure if he's going to come for me, not after the way things ended between us, but a part of me hopes he will, and that's enough for me to lie to the bastards in front of me.

I barely finish the thought when I hear a sound coming from directly behind us. The illuminating moon in the sky casts a dim light over us, and I catch a glimpse of a large figure moving behind Xander's father.

Everything seems to happen so fast. One second, I am standing, and the next, I'm crouching down on the ground. Gunshots start going off around me, the thud of bodies hitting the ground fills my ears, and the metallic smell of blood fills my nostrils. I flatten myself to the cold patio pavement, trying to stay out of the gunfire. The last thing I need is to get shot. My gaze swings around but it's so dark and there is blood everywhere. It's hard to make out what is going on, and who is who.

I know I should feel terror, that I should probably run, but I can't bring myself to move. I'm frozen in place, caught in the crossfire.

I peek up through strawberry-blonde locks and spot Xander's father on his knees, holding his side. Agony contorts his devilish features. Blood is already soaking through his shirt and spilling out between his fingers like a river flooding over its banks.

A warm hand lands gently against my back, making my head snap to the side. I roll to my back and slash at the hand touching me.

"It's me. Damon. Are you okay?" Concern catches in his voice.

I shake my head, realizing it's really Damon kneeling beside me, and not some figment of my imagination. "I think so." My lips tremble. "Is Xander here?"

I can see the ghosting of a smile on Damon's lips. "Of course, he's here. How do you think I got here?"

I grimace. "I didn't know if he would come for me."

Gunshots ring out, peppering the air, and Damon and I remain on the ground for another second before someone in the distance yells, "All clear."

Then he's grabbing me and hauling me up with him, pulling me away from their father. He drags me with him until I'm on the opposite side of the house, protected from any stray bullets.

"Stay here until Xander or I come to get you," he demands, before shoving a gun into my hand. "Point and shoot at anyone you don't know."

I open my mouth to say something, but he's gone, disappearing around the corner before I get a chance to. I hold the warm gun in my shaking hands, ready to kill anyone who crosses my path.

20

Xander

THE METALLIC SMELL of blood and gunpowder coats the air. Watching them manhandle Ella the way they did has me unhinged. I kill without thought, bullet after bullet entering man after man's brain. I don't think, I simply act. My only thought at that moment is to kill and protect what is mine.

I kill every single bastard here, and then move toward my father, who Damon already shot. I know Ella isn't far from where my father is right at this moment, on his knees bleeding out. If she wasn't here to think about, I would make this very slow and painful for him. But I don't want to draw it out any longer than I have to, not when I have to think about getting her out of here and to a doctor.

I will have to satisfy my need by looking him in the eyes when he takes his last breath. It is good enough to know that I am taking his life and everything he ever worked for with it. Damon comes around the corner and our eyes meet. It's time to end this shit, once for all.

I walk up to my father, who is already bleeding out on the ground. He is wheezing heavily, trying to get air in his lungs, but the gurgling sound he's making tells me that all he's doing is sucking in a whole lot of blood.

"Did you really think you'd get away with taking her from me?" I snarl, smacking him in the back of the head with my gun.

He doesn't say a word, nor do I want him to. I'm sure he can't talk around the blood rising in his throat even if he wanted to. His eyes pierce mine. They're cold, vacant, and even as he's on his way to dying, he still doesn't show a shred of remorse or compassion.

"Did you really think this could end any other way? You might've faked your death last time, but you won't get that lucky this time. Today, you're fucking dying."

Damon holds his gun in his hands, his finger on the trigger. Even after everything my father did to me, after the way he hurt my Mouse... I'm still giving this to him. He deserves to be the one to end our father.

Damon looks at me. "Let's do it together, brother."

No longer are we two little boys facing the abuse of our father. Now we're two powerful men, making the one man who was supposed to protect us from all the bad in world pay the ultimate price.

I smirk. "Fuck, yeah."

I position myself next to my brother. Together, we point our guns at our father's head. Right before the trigger is pulled, I think I see a flicker of emotion in our father's eyes.

Damon pulls the trigger and then I pull my own. Our father's head snaps back as the front of his skull is torn apart by the bullets. His body hits the ground a moment later, and I feel like all my fears have vanished.

Finally, we are free. Free from the darkness, the pain, the anger. I savor the moment for a few minutes, just looking at the dead body before us with my brother by my side. Everything around us has gone quiet, all the gunfire ceased, and a peacefulness washes over me. My mind slips back to the present, and I feel the need to go to Mouse. To apologize and beg for her forgiveness.

"Where is she?" I ask Damon, who looks like he is deep in thought.

"Around the house, I gave her a gun, so you better announce yourself," Damon warns and points me in the direction to go.

I start walking toward my mouse, wondering if she even wants to see me right now. I fucking hurt her, almost killed her, threw her in the cell and basically handed her to my father when she did nothing wrong.

Guilt settles so deep inside of me I know I will never fully be able to let go of this. She could've died tonight, and that's my fucking fault. She proved herself to me, earned my trust, and I didn't even let her speak. I didn't let her tell me what happened. I didn't let her defend herself, and I know I will carry this guilt with me until I take my last breath, no matter how long my life might be and regardless of whether she forgives me or not. I walk around the side of the house, stopping only when I see a small body leaning against the siding.

"It's me, don't shoot." I hold my hands up and take a step closer to her. "Unless you want to shoot me. In that case go ahead, I won't hold it against you. I definitely deserve it."

Mouse comes toward me and for a split second, I think she might actually shoot me, I wouldn't try and stop her if she did, but then she drops the gun to the ground and runs straight for me. Her small body slams into mine, and her slim arms snake around my middle.

I shouldn't be happy. I know this, but I am. I'm happy to have her back, to be rid of my father. I know I can love and be loved in return. I hold her close to my body, kissing the top of her head. "I'm so fucking sorry, Mouse. So fucking sorry. I fucked up. I hurt you. I ruined everything."

"I didn't think you would come for me. I thought I would never see you again. I thought you hated me and that I'd become your father's whore." She starts sobbing into my chest, and every single word is like another stab to my heart. I failed her in every possible way, and there is no forgetting that.

I pull back slightly and grip her by the chin. I need her to hear and see me when I say these words to her. "I swear to you, Ella. If you forgive me, I will be a better man. I will care for you, and I will protect and cherish you." I stare deeply into her eyes, hoping she can see how much I mean every single word I am saying.

"I should have fucking trusted you. I should have believed in you. I told you that I loved you and when it came time to prove myself, I failed you. I failed *us*, but it will never happen again. Never."

Mouse shakes her head as if she doesn't believe me. "I still love you, Xander. I know I probably shouldn't, but I do. I can't help it. I love you, I love Q, and I'll love..." She trails off, her face falling.

"I love you, too, Mouse, and I'm going to love this baby, *our* baby." I release my hold on her chin and move my hand between us and over her still-flat belly, which will soon be swollen with our child. I can't wait to see her full with our baby. I'll bet she looks just as sexy pregnant as she does now.

"You found the test?" Surprise colors her features, and for a moment, I wonder if she was trying to hide it from me. I wouldn't be surprised if she was. I didn't exactly treat Q's mother with respect or kindness when I found out she was having him, but this was different. I wanted Mouse; I didn't want the woman my father had sent to me.

"Yes, I came down to the cell as soon as I found it, and that's when I realized you were gone."

Mouse frowns. "I didn't have time to look at the test because your men came in, but I knew I was. I felt it deep in my chest. I was going to tell you, of course, but I wanted to be sure first."

"I know. I never really expected you to hide it from me, and even if you did, I wouldn't blame you. My relationship with Q's mom was nothing like the one I have with you. I'd never hurt you like that... never," I assure her, because yes, I've treated her horribly, hurt her many times, and there aren't any accuses for that behavior. But now that I know what it feels like to lose her, I will never do anything to risk her life again.

"Right now, I just want to get you home, get you showered, and have Doctor Brown come in and check on you." My hands tremble as they trace over her features.

Sadness and guilt flicker in her blue eyes, and those two emotions mixed together frighten the hell out of me.

"Do you... do you want to come home with me still?"

I don't know what I'll do if she says no, but I would learn to deal with it. I can figure out how to give her some space if that's what she needs. However, if she tells me she doesn't want to see me again, I'll probably have to take her hostage all over again.

"I do. I want to come with you... but I'm going to need some time... and space. I need more freedom, and I need you to trust me, because after all of this, trust is something we need to work on." Her eyes skirt from mine. "And I want to see my sister..."

I try my hardest to hide the hurt from my eyes, but this fucking kills me. It hurts so fucking bad I might as well have shot myself in the chest. But if this is what she needs, then I'll give it to her. If she wants space and time for us to work on things, I will make it happen.

I'll give her what she wants, for as long as I can.

"Whatever you want, Mouse, and you can see your sister whenever you want. I know where she is, and she is safe."

"She is?" Her eyes light up.

"Yes, I've seen her briefly. She looked fine, happy even." I've seen my Mouse cry many times but never with tears of joy. She is so happy hearing about her sister, and I am more than fucking glad that I could at least give her this happiness.

"I'm not going to give up on you, on us. I'm sorry for everything, for hurting you, for fucking up." I wish she could feel the pain I feel over hurting her. "I'll do whatever I can to prove that to you every single day from here on out."

"I know you will, Xander. You're a good man, even if you don't think so." She pats a hand to my chest and presses a kiss to my cheek. Tears fill her eyes, making the blue seem darker. She shivers, and I pull away, shrugging out of my jacket. I drape it over her slender shoulders.

"Hate to break up the show, but I really want to get home to my wife." Damon's voice interrupts the silence.

I nod curtly, understanding completely where he's coming from now. If Mouse wasn't here with me right now, then I'd be headed right back into her arms.

"Let's get you back to the house and cleaned up," I whisper into her hair, telling myself that I can do this. I can be the man she needs me to be. Now that my father's dead, I can let go of the darkness, of the pain. I can find happiness with Mouse and show her the same love she's shown me even when I wasn't worthy of being loved by her.

21

Ella

"Your blood pressure is good. You have some bruising as well as some cuts and scrapes but you're in good health. Drink plenty of water and get some rest. I'll come in another four weeks to check on you and the baby. If you have any problems before that, just give me a ring and I'll be over." Doc Brown gives me a gentle smile and packs up his stuff.

We are in the guest bedroom where I slept last night, since Xander apparently *renovated* his bedroom. Silence blankets the room, and Xander doesn't say anything even after the doctor walks out of the room, leaving us alone in the bedroom. Instead, he remains seated beside me, his hand holding mine. I wonder if me telling him I wanted a break, some space, hurt him?

"Are you okay, Xander?" I prod quietly. It had only been twenty-four-hours since Xander saved my life and killed his father.

During those hours, he'd been mostly quiet, answering only questions that I asked, or engaging in conversation if I started it.

"I'm fine, Mouse. I just want to do the right thing. I want to be the man that you're proud to have as yours."

I was an emotional wreck, and everything he said seemed to turn the water works on. Sitting up on the bed, I dangle my feet over the edge while facing him. "I'm not leaving you, Xander. I just need some space. Some time to digest everything."

"I know," he responds, a sadness trickling into his voice.

"Then why're you acting like I'm leaving you?"

Xander doesn't respond. Instead, he pushes from his chair and comes to stand in front of me, pushing my thighs apart, before moving between them. I'm in nothing but one of his t-shirts, and the fabric rises up as he does so, exposing my bare pussy.

"I don't deserve you, Mouse. Not even a fucking little bit, but I can't risk losing you." He gently nudges me backward, and I fall helplessly against the bed sheets.

"You aren't losing me," I whisper.

Xander gently pushes my t-shirt up over my belly, his warm lips press against my skin and I damn near moan in pleasure.

"Good, because I'm going to make this up to you. I'm going to go slow with you, Mouse. I'm going to love every inch of you. I'm going to show you what it's like to be cherished. I'm going to please and care for you as you did me."

Lifting a hand, I run it through his silky black hair as his lips move over my heated skin. His kisses promise ungodly pleasure as they move lower, and lower, making my head spin with need, and my belly pool with desire.

"Xander." His name comes out as a moan, and I'm not sure if we should be doing this. I don't want him to stop but I don't want him to think I'm going to have sex with him. I'm not ready for that yet. He just killed his dad, and I just found out we're having a baby.

"Shhh, Mouse, I don't want anything from you. I just want to please you, to give you pleasure, can I do that? Can I pleasure you?" He drops down to his knees between my legs and looks up at me, eyes the color of the night sky.

A part of me wants to tell him no, but deep down, I know I want this. I want his touch. I want... no, I *need* to feel close to him. So, I nod, giving him my approval, and whimper when he lifts my legs, placing them over his shoulders.

He opens me up wider, his fingers digging into my thighs. I feel his heated breath against my mound, and then his fingers as he trails them up and down the inside of my thighs.

"So ripe and ready for me." His voice is filled with want, need, and my fingers find their way into his hair, pulling him forward.

"I want you," I gasp, feeling one of his thick fingers slip inside my tightness.

"Is this what you want, baby? Me to fuck you with my fingers?"

I can't respond, not with his finger inside me. He slides in until he's knuckle-deep and keeps himself seated while flicking his tongue against my swollen bundle of nerves. How I feel so full with nothing but his finger inside of me, I don't know, but I want more of him, all of him.

A warmth fills my veins and works its way up every inch of flesh. Xander ravages me, feasting on my pussy as if he is starved. I can feel every swipe of his tongue, every suck and flick pushes me closer to that breaking point of pure bliss.

"Xander... oh, god... oh, god..." One of my hands fists into the bed sheets while the other holds him head in place. My legs fall apart, giving him even more room. I cling to the pleasure spiraling out of control inside of me.

"Come for me, beautiful. Come all over my tongue. I want to taste you inside my mouth." If it's not his words that are going to push me over the edge, it's his finger moving in and out of me. Without warning, he pulls away, leaving my swollen clit all alone. I whimper, wanting his tongue right back on that sensitive bundle of nerves.

What I get instead is a second finger added to the first, stretching me, owning me, as he pumps in and out of my tightness, giving me just enough pressure while stroking all the right spots. I feel Xander's heated gaze on mine, and I push up onto my elbows, feeling the need to watch him own my body.

He moves in and out of me with pure precision and need, his muscles tighten and hunger for my body as he continues to bring me toward the edge. It's enough to send me into a freefall of pleasure. My peak finds me, and hits me deep, right in the center of my chest, moving downward.

"Xander," I cry out, as the first wave slams into me. Pleasure unravels like a bow that's been untied, the ribbons blowing in the wind. My eyes drift closed, and my pussy clenches around his fingers. I feel him slowly moving them in and out of me, milking every single drop of my release out of me.

He leans forward and presses a kiss to my belly, his sweaty forward resting against my clammy skin for a moment. Air fills my lungs, and my pulse pounds in my ears as the endorphins of pleasure run rampant through my veins.

"Fuck, Mouse, you came so hard... so fucking hard. I wish it was my cock inside you instead of my fingers."

"I'll... if you need..." I hadn't ever offered to give him a blowjob, not on my own. Usually he asked me, but this time, I wanted to ask him. I wanted to return the favor.

But Xander refused, shaking his head. "No. That's not how this works. Let me pleasure you. Let me show you how much I want this, how much I want you, and then, when I've lived up to your expectations and done what I need to do, then you can give to me."

"But you do all those—"

Xander places a finger against my lips, shushing me. "No. Don't make excuses for me. I need to be a better man. For you, for Q, for our unborn baby. I need to be the man I should've been all along."

I don't say anything, because there is nothing to say. Xander wants to prove himself. He wants to make things right, and I want that, too. I don't want to give into him simply because we're having a baby together. I know he has demons and skeletons in his closet, but I want a real relationship. I want us to be together, and though I'm not going anywhere, I feel like we need to work on trusting each other.

"I love you, Mouse. I didn't want to believe that I could, but I do. I love every single fucking thing about you. I loved you even when I knew I shouldn't. You deserve better, and I'll be damned if I let you settle for less than perfect."

"I love you, too, Xander." I smile, enjoying this new side of him.

He pulls my shirt back down, covering my bare skin and helps me move back onto the mattress. Once I'm situated beneath the covers, he crawls in beside me, tucking me into his side, his boner poking into my back. I'm blanketed in warmth, and I feel secure, and happier than I ever have been in my entire life.

"Someday, I will be good enough to marry you, and you'll be the best fucking wife and mother to our children the world could ever have."

I blink away the tears that appear in my eyes. Xander protected me when he didn't have to. Yes, he hurt me, and broke me at times but how could I expect any less from a man who never knew what love was? From a man who never experienced what it was like to be cared for. Xander only knew death and pain, and me coming into his life opened up doors he had never thought of touching.

He thought having a son was weakness.

He thought finding someone to love him was a weakness. And maybe when his father was alive it was, but now, now it was a blessing and no matter what, I was going to remind him of how much of a blessing it was every single day.

"Someday, I'm going to marry you, Xander, and you'll be the best father and husband a woman could ever ask for." My voice cracks, giving my emotions away. I feel Xander melt into my body, and I relish in the feeling of being in his arms again.

"I don't deserve you, Ella, but I'll be fucking damned if I let anyone else have you. You're mine, forever, and always. I'll be keeping you until the day I die."

As my eyes drift closed, a permanent smile appears on my lips, one that I know will linger there far beyond today, tomorrow, or a month from now.

EPILOGUE

*X*ander

Six Months Later

I GIVE every single one of my men the night off. I have the nanny upstairs in Q's bedroom for the rest of the evening, and I'm ready to show my sweet little mouse how good of a chef I am. I haven't cooked but a few times before, but I want to be this man for her. I've worked at it every single day. Taking anger management classes and talking about my feelings more. It made me feel like a fucking pussy, but I did it for her.

I did it because it's what she deserves and what my children deserve. Darkness still surrounds me, but I don't let it claim me, not like I let it before. I still kill, but I do it for the greater good instead of just doing it because I can.

I will never let the darkness ruin my life like it did with my father's, and I tell myself this every single day.

"Are you ready for dinner?"

Mouse looks up from reading her book at my question. "Isn't it a little early for dinner?" She smiles up at me, her big blues sparkling with happiness. Her beautiful strawberry-blonde hair flows freely down her back.

"Well, yes, but I still have to cook it, so if I start it now, it'll be ready in time for dinner."

Mouse raises her eyebrows at me. "You... cook?"

"Of course, I cook." I grin. "Do you want to come down to the kitchen with me or do you want me to come and get you when I'm done cooking?"

"Oh, no, sir. I'm coming. I've got to see this for myself." She puts the book down on the little side table and pushes herself up and off the armrest of the recliner I got her. Her belly is nice and round now and because of her petite frame, she looks as if she is farther along than seven months. She's starting to wobble when she walks, too, and it's the cutest fucking thing I've ever seen.

If I have it my way, I'll have her pregnant forever, just because she looks so fucking sexy swollen with our child. She loops her arm into mine, and we walk downstairs together. It doesn't take her but a few steps to notice that something is up.

"Where are all the guards?" she asks curiously.

"I gave everybody the night off." I shrug nonchalantly, because really, it's not a big deal.

"You did?" She looks around like she is expecting a guard to pop out and scare her.

We get to the kitchen where I've already set out all the ingredients for parmesan chicken. It's not a gourmet meal, but that's not the point. It's not about making something over the top or expensive. It's just about creating a meal for the woman I love.

I guide Mouse to a chair, and she sits down, watching me intently as I fill the pot for the pasta with water, salting it I put it on the stove. I move around the kitchen with ease, as if I've done it all my life. I grab a knife and start cutting the chicken breast into smaller pieces.

I feel so domesticated, and it's all because of the beautiful fucking woman sitting across from me.

"Do you want me to help you? I mean, I kinda miss cooking. I haven't done it in what seems like forever."

"You can join me if you'd like, and as you know, you're welcome to cook whenever you want."

She smiles and gets up and walks around the kitchen island, coming to stand beside me.

She pours breadcrumbs into a bowl and makes an egg wash in another before taking the cut-up chicken from me. I wash and dry my hands after cutting up all the chicken.

I know I should probably turn around and preheat the oven, but I can't help but step behind her. I snake my arms around her body, resting my hands on top of her round belly. She leans against my chest, her head resting against my shoulder.

She smells of brown sugar and vanilla, like a perfectly cooked dessert that I just want to devour but savor all at once.

"Is this the kind of normal you were talking about, Mouse? Because I could get used to this," I whisper into her hair.

"Yes, I like having you all to myself. I like us being just a normal couple. I want to go baby shopping and on dates."

"We'll make this happen more often, I promise. Someday, we might not even need guards. It will just be you, me, Q, and Adela, and maybe one or two more little ones."

"You want more children?" Her tone tells me she is surprised.

"Of course. Have you seen how beautiful you are? Now that I've seen you like this, I don't think I can imagine you being anything but swollen with our children."

"You do make cute babies," she giggles. "But I don't know about staying pregnant my whole life. I'm miserable right now, and we still have another two months to go."

"How about we take it one day at a time." I kiss the back of her head and she sighs into my touch. She's so reactive to my touch, to my love, and I know that she is meant to be mine.

We finish cooking together. Our movements are synchronized, as if we both belong and work in the kitchen together every night preparing dinner, and maybe, someday, we will. If I can let go of the control, let go of the crippling fear of someone hurting my family... maybe then, someday, somehow, we can live a normal life.

I guide Mouse over to the leather couch, and we snuggle together. We talk about how Violet is putting the baby shower together, and all the things Mouse still needs to get. I remind myself to take her shopping, just her and I at least once more before our baby girl gets here.

I get the chicken out of the oven and prepare two plates. We eat together, just the two of us in a quiet house. When we're done eating, Mouse gets up and grabs her plate as if she is about to clear the table. I take the plate from her hand and motion for her to sit back down.

"Don't worry about that right now. The dishes can wait. Come on, I want to show you something." I deposit the plates onto the counter before I take Mouse's hand and lead her out to the patio in the backyard. The summer air is still sticky with heat, but it's starting to cool off. It's the perfect kind of weather to spend a little time outside.

As soon as we walk through the French doors and out onto the patio, Mouse sees what I did to it.

She gasps as if in shock, bringing a hand to her chest. "Xander... what is all of this?"

"You like it?"

She stares at the bed of oversized pillows and blankets covering the makeshift bed. I've strung some outdoor lights above it and vases filled with flowers are placed all around the area.

Tealights are nestled into little bowls of water, placed all over the patio, and with the moon hanging in the sky, it makes the entire place look just as romantic as I'd hoped it would.

"It's beautiful, Xander!" Tears fill her beautiful blue eyes, and I wipe them away with my thumbs as they slip down her cheeks.

"No crying, Mouse. Tonight is special to me, and not just because you're here with me. It's special because I've made the decision to let love win, forever, and always. I vowed I'd always protect you, and there's one more way I can ensure they you will always be protected and cared for."

Mouse blinks very slowly, as if she isn't sure what's going to happen next.

The weight of the ring in my pocket feels heavy now.

What if she says no?

Things have been great between us but there is still a chance she might say no.

The thought never occurred to me until now. I'd been working on my emotions, dealing with the pain and anger I had. I'd given her space like she'd asked, and we'd grown closer with each passing day, but what if this wasn't what she wanted?

"Are you okay? You look like you might be sick?" Mouse's features fill with concern. I wanted to laugh... even in these moments she proved how sweet, and caring she was.

"I've never wanted someone the way I want you, Mouse."

She nods, as if she understands but she has no clue. She has no fucking clue how hard her presence makes my heart beat, or how much her whimpers and pleas during sex push me over the edge. She has no clue what she does to me and maybe that's how it's supposed to be with us.

"I love you, Xander, but you didn't have to do any of this." Her hands gesture toward the lights and bed.

"Oh, but I did..." I grin, reaching into my pocket. I pull out the red velvet box and drop down onto one knee before her while flipping open the top. As soon as she realizes what's happening, her hands cover her mouth. Her gaze widens with excitement and shock.

"Will you do me the honor of becoming Mrs. Rossi, Mouse?"

"Do you... do you really mean it?" The words rush from her lips, and my smile widens.

"Yes, I really mean it. I want you to be my wife."

And just like that, she is crying again. Big huge wet tears fall from her eyes, and she hiccups into her hand before nodding.

I reach out, taking her hand in mine.

I had her ring custom made. A two-carat diamond sitting on a white gold band. Thanks to Violet, I didn't have to guess her ring size. I slide it onto her slender ring finger... and damn near sigh finding that it fits her perfectly.

As I try to stand back up, Mouse takes my face between her hands and brings her lips to mine. I wrap my arms around her and pull her closer... as close I can get her without squishing her belly.

She tastes delicious, and I want nothing more than to strip her bare and taste more of her, every single inch of her flesh. My tongue delves between her lips, and she grips onto me tighter, her hands fisting into my shirt and showing me just how much she wants this.

I pull away, resting my forehead against hers, my body trembling. "I want you, Mouse. Can I have you? Can I make love to you beneath the stars?"

Mouse's deep blue eyes peer up at me. "Yes... yes, please," she exclaims, taking a step back, gripping the hem of her dress, and pulling it up and over her head. The fabric falls to the ground, and she giggles softly, standing before me in nothing more than a white pair of panties and bra. It's nothing over the top, no lace, or silk, just plain white panties and a matching bra.

Her stomach is swollen, and her tits are huge, heaving with each breath she takes. Her cheeks turn an adorable shade of pink, and I start undressing myself, tossing every piece of clothing to the ground.

When I'm in nothing more than my briefs, she reaches for me, guiding us toward the makeshift bed. I lean over her, kissing her, giving to her every single emotion she draws out of me.

Once she's melting beneath my fingers, I peel her panties off her and gaze down at her glistening pussy. She's ready for me, more than ready.

"You look so fucking beautiful right now. Like I'm truly the luckiest bastard in the world to have you." I don't give her a chance to respond. Instead, I sink between her creamy thighs, nudging them apart so I can fit perfectly between them.

Then I feast. Her taste explodes against my tongue, and I grip her hips, holding her in place, licking and sucking at her sweet pussy. She whimpers, and her fingers sink into my hair, pulling at the locks, sending rivulets of pleasure down my spine.

"Xander... I'm... I'm coming..." she cries out, and I swirl my tongue around her tight entrance, dipping in and out until I feel her explode. I lap up her release and kick out of my boxers. Tonight, I want my queen to be in control. I want her to own me like she has every day since I fucking met her.

"Come here, Mouse," I order, helping her sit up. She looks slightly confused but listens to me. I sink down onto the mattress right where she just was and stroke my already stiff cock up and down. She gazes down at me, her white teeth sinking into her plump bottom lip seductively.

"Sit on the throne, my queen."

Mouse shakes her head, a tiny giggle escaping her lips. She moves down to her knees and crawls across the bed. Once she reaches me, she tosses one leg over mine, straddling me. I grip her hips and help her lower herself onto my thickness. We both moan in unison as her pussy swallows my cock inch by glorious inch.

When she is fully seated and my whole dick has disappeared into her tightness, I gaze into her eyes. I pepper kisses against her collarbone, throat, and chest before unclasping her bra. As soon as I do, her heavy tits spring free. I take one of her stiff pink nipples into my mouth and swirl my tongue around it while sucking on it gently. Mouse arches her back and pushes her tits farther into my face.

My hands roam over her body, touching and caressing every inch of her silky-smooth skin. She starts to rock her hips back and forth, grinding onto me while I give each of her breasts equal attention.

Her movements are unsure and a bit uncoordinated at first, but fuck, this feels too good to stop. I'm so deep inside of her I can feel my tip at the end of channel. And the view of having her sit on top of me is unbelievable, her tits right in my face, begging to be sucked.

She keeps moving and starts to set a rhythm. She moves more confidently after a few minutes, and I let her set the pace, let her take from me whatever she wants.

"Fuck, Mouse, you feel so good. Ride my cock, use me however you want." My words seem to egg her on, as she picks up speed, her nails digging into my chest as her pants and moans grow louder and more erratic. She bounces up and down, and I pull her into my chest, holding her there tightly while I thrust my hips upward, deep inside her.

Sweat beads against my forehead, and the summer heat clings to my skin. Mouse mumbles some words that don't make sense, but I hear my name somewhere in the mix. Her pants turn into gasps as she grinds into me furiously, her hips moving in at a relentless pace. Finally, her pussy clenches around me, her walls squeezing my cock so hard and tight that my own orgasm starts to build. Gripping her hips with bruising force, I thrust upward a few more times before my balls tighten and draw together.

Pleasure consumes me, zinging through every nerve ending in my body. I can't tell what is up, or down, only that everything starts and ends with this tiny woman in my arms. I groan loudly as I empty myself into her depth. I feel her pussy spasm around me, drawing out both our orgasms. Mouse sighs, and I sit us up a little bit so I can hold her against my chest without squishing her round belly.

"I love you, Mousey." I cup her by the cheek, understanding and seeing the beauty in love now. She showed me this. She gave me one of the greatest gifts of all.

"Good, because I'm keeping you." She gives me a sleepy smile before snuggling into my chest. I tip my head up to the sky, looking at all the twinkling stars above us, wondering if life can get any better than this. She lets her body fall to the side, and I lay her down next to me gently. Then I grab a blanket from beside me and toss it over us.

"Yeah, I'm keeping you, too, Mouse."

∼

Thank You for reading Keep Me.
If you loved Keep Me make sure you pick up a copy of
GUARD ME
Keep reading for a sneak peak!

CR
BOOK THREE

GUARD *me*

USA TODAY BESTSELLING AUTHORS

J.L. BECK &
C. HALLMAN

PROLOGUE
Violet

The music pounds loudly in my ears. It's so loud I can't hear myself think let alone, hear whatever it is my best friend is trying to say to me. I don't know why I was so excited about coming here for my birthday. It seemed like such a good idea when my friend's suggested it.

However, now that I'm here everything seems so much less appealing. My ears hurt from the loud music, and my throat is scratchy from the smoke that clings to the air. The skin tight dress and black high heels I'm wearing are getting more uncomfortable with each passing minute. All in all coming here was a shit idea.

Sweat beads against my forehead, as I survey the crowd. Everyone here seems to be way older than me. I'm only eighteen but this club allows people under twenty-one to come in as long as you let them stamp both of your hands.

Some older guys offered to buy me a drink a couple minutes ago and I'm starting to wonder if maybe I should have let him. I really don't want to get drunk in here and lose my wits, but it's so hot, and I can't help but wonder if I'd loosen up with a little alcohol in my system.

I grip onto my cell phone tightly in my hands deciding there won't be any drinking for me tonight. I'll just call Ella and have her pick me up. She's going to be pissed at me for not telling her what I was doing but she'll get over it, she always does. I unlock my phone and start scrolling through my messages when a man appears at my side.

"Here." He says shoving a glass at me. It has some red colored liquid in it and I know better than to take some drink from a random stranger. I shake my head and hold up my hand to motion to him that I am not interested but he just shoves the glass closer to my face.

Annoyance boils deep inside me. I take the glass, hoping it will make the asshole leave. I don't take a sip, neither do I plan to.

"Want to dance?" The guy leans into me and slurs right next to my ear. He smells of smoke, and sweat and I almost gag at the mixture of scents.

"No, thank you." I decline politely.

"But I just bought you a drink, the least you can do is dance with me." He gives me a creepy smile, and I shudder attempting to take a step backward. The entire place is packed, bodies rubbing against each other, making it hard to escape this asshole.

Thinking smart I know I need to find another way to get away from him. My eyes glance over a neon restroom sign off in the distance.

"You right, I'm just going to the bathroom really quick and then I'll dance with you." I give him a wide smile and set the drink on the table a few feet away from us.

"Alright, I'll be waiting right here for you baby." He slurs, as I start to walk away.

Walking in the direction of the bathroom, I weave between people, pushing and shoving just to get a step ahead. Once I reach the restrooms I turn and start walking back towards the entrance of the club. Music vibrates through me, and I find it harder and harder to breathe with all the bodies around me. I'll just go outside and call Ella, that way maybe I can tell her I wanted to go to the club but changed my mind. Her shift at the diner will be over in a few minutes, so she'll be able to swing by here on her way back to the apartment.

Then we can forget like tonight never happened.

I make it through the crowd and walk into the hallway leading outside. There are only a few people lingering near the exit. Nobody seems to be paying me an ounce of attention, all except one man. He is leaning against the far wall, his entire body encased in the shadows, but I can see his eyes scanning me up and down. He's staring at my body in a way that makes me feel exposed and I don't like it, not one bit. I make my feet walk faster as I hurry past him, his gaze remaining on me the whole time. As I pass him the hair on the back of my neck stands up, and a bad feeling fills my gut. This guy is pure evil... it oozes out of him, like a bad smell. I can feel it, see it.

The moment I step outside and fresh air fills my lungs I feel a little better. I peer up into the night sky, pressing against the brick exterior wall of the club. I flip my phone around in my sweaty hand to call my sister, but when I scroll down to her name and hit send I realize that I have no signal.

Shit.

I start walking down the sidewalk holding the phone up in front of me hoping to find a spot where I get at least one bar. I take little steps, watching the phone screen more than my surroundings.

"Shit," I mumble to myself, knowing I'm going to get my ass chewed whenever I do get ahold of Ella.

"Need a lift?" A unfamiliar voice calls out, making me jump. I quickly turn around dropping my phone in the process. It's the creepy guy from the hallway, and now he is standing a few inches away from me.

My voice is stuck in my throat, and all I can do is shake my head no. The man gives me a sinister smile that has my stomach coiling with nervous knots. Looking past his shoulders I realize that I've wandered away a good bit from the front of the club and, that now I'm completely alone with this unknown man. My heart rate spikes as fear surge through my veins. I don't know how, or why but I just know something bad is about to happen.

I take a step back, desperately trying to get some distance between him and I. I feel paranoid like I'm losing my mind. I think he is going to grab me but he makes no move to do so. I take another step back and he smiles at me, his eyes darken as if he is enjoying this little cat and mouse game.

I take one small step backward realizing then why he didn't try and grab me. A set of strong arms wrap around me from behind. Fear and panic creeps in when a large hand covers my mouth stopping the scream burning to escape from my lips. I start kicking and flailing my arms, attempting to hit any appendage I can.

Time seems to stand still when I feel a prick in the side of my neck.

I fight for another five seconds before my limbs get heavy and my eyes close without permission. I'm vaguely aware of a car pulling up next to us and my body being thrown into it like a rag doll. I want to fight, scream, and cry, but my body is completely useless and not following any of my commands. I feel my mind drifting away as panic settles deep inside of me. My last thought before the darkness completely claims me is if I will ever wake up again.

∽

CHAPTER ONE
Violet

I groan into the air, my eyelids feeling as if they have been replaced with sandpaper. My head is pounding making it hard for me to think...I shiver as a coldness sweeps over my exposed skin. Exhaling I pry my eyes open and find that I'm lying in a bed looking at a white ceiling.

For a moment, I think I'm at the hospital.

Was I in an accident?

I turn my head expecting to find an IV sticking out of my arm, or some type of medical equipment. What I see instead has my heart stopping mid-beat. A deep panic settles into my bones sinking deep into my core. I'm in a concrete box. There are no windows, in fact, all four walls are white, with no paintings or decor.

It is a completely empty room minus the mattress beneath me. I scurry into a sitting position, pressing my back against the wall. It's cold, and I stifle a whimper by biting my lip. My eyes move over the room once more.

The mattress beneath me is stained and doesn't even have a sheet on it. There is no blanket or pillow. Nothing about this room says I'll be staying for a while, and that terrifies me. If whoever has me doesn't plan on keeping me for a while then that means... I can't even finish the thought without feeling like I might pass out.

I look down at myself. I'm wearing nothing but a damn skin tight dress, and my shoes are long gone. Looking at my attire jogs a memory from my mind. I remember...*my birthday...the club...that creepy, scary guy.* Everything comes rushing back to me all at once.

Oh god no, where am I? What happened to me?

My gaze swings around the room again. I have to find a way out. There seems to be only one exit and entrance out of the room and it's through the large metal door on the far side of the room. I eye the thing, knowing there is no way I'll be able to break it down or get it open. There is a small door in the center of it that reminds me of a food slot of a prison cell door.

Next to the door is a large mirror set inside the wall. I eye it with apprehension. I can't help but wonder if it's just a mirror or one-way mirrors, where people can watch you from the other side. There is another room off to the right of the room, that leads into a small bathroom. I slowly stand on wobbly likes to take a closer look inside of it.

"Shit," I grumble when my bare feet touch the cold cement floor. It's impossibly cold in this room and I've never craved for a blanket more in my life then I do right now.

Inside the tiny bathroom are a toilet and a sink. There is no toilet paper, soap, or any of the things that a normal person would have in their own bathroom at home. I back out of the tiny room, feeling more unsure than I did before I stepped foot inside of it. I scurry over to the mattress, crawling across it, before sitting down in the furthest corner, pulling my legs up to my chest. I'm cold, so cold.

Times seems to blend together. I don't know how long I sit like this, could be hours, or minutes, maybe even days. There is no real way of telling time here...my eyes start to droop closed again when I hear something happening in front of my door.

I jump up and run to it. I hear the rattling of keys followed by a lock opening. I want to scream, beg, plead...but apart of me is terrified to find out what is on the other side of that door.

Disappointment fills my veins when instead of the large metal door opening, the small flap to the little door inside of the door opens and a plate is shoved inside the room.

"Hello?" I call out, my voice coming out scratchy and raw. "Please, you don't have to help me, but please tell me why am I here? Tell me who took me," I beg and get down on my knees hoping to catch a glimpse of the outside world through the tiny opening.

My pleas go unanswered and the door quickly slams shut, nearly knocking the paper plate onto the floor. I eye the sandwich and the bottle of water that's now all the floor in front of the door. Tears build up in my eyes and threaten to spill over as I make my way back to the mattress leaving the plate of food. Stomach tightens nervously, there is no way I could keep anything down right now.

I don't know how many days pass, all I know that I am on the verge of insanity. If I'm not sleeping, I'm crying and when I'm not doing either of those things I'm driving myself insane while trying to figure out why I am where I am.

Every time a meal is brought I try and talk to the person on the other side of the door, but as always they don't respond. I've stopped eating the food they bring in hopes that someone will be forced to come in and talk to me. My eyes often go to the mirror that overlooks the room. Sometimes I get the feeling that I'm being watched and I most likely am since I'm almost certain the damn thing is not just a mirror. I remain on the mattress, just as I always do, attempting to get warm. I'm so cold, I'm not sure I remember what it feels like to be warm anymore. The little thin dress I'm wearing gives me little to no protection, or warmth and I shiver uncontrollably.

Between being cold and always afraid of the unknown I get little to no sleep. I'm in a constant state of panic, my body is so stiff and exhausted that even tiny movements cause my muscles to ache. I wonder if my sister is looking for me, searching for me? I wonder where I am? Who took me? There are a million questions running through my mind, and no answers to turn too. I shiver against the mattress, my head perks up at a noise outside my door.

My last meal of the day was brought a few hours ago...and this has never happened before. I hear the jingling of keys and deep husky laughter...laughter that belongs to men.

God no. My entire body clams up, when the door opens, a loud creak vibrating through the room. I look up, paralyzed with fear as two dark-haired men enter the room.

"My oh my, look what we have here Luca." The two men walk unsteadily on their feet towards me. I can smell the alcohol on their breath and there still a few feet away from me.

I've wished for the door to open for so long, hating that it kept me trapped in this room, but what I didn't know was that it protected me, shielded me, because now that it's open I want it to close, taking the two men before me with it.

"Look at those full lips, I bet they will look great around my cock," the other man snickers.

"How angry do you think Ivan will be if we pop her cherry?" The first man asks. Fear like I've never felt before spirals out of control inside of me. They edge closer towards me, and I wish the wall would swallow me whole, making me disappear from this room and out of reach from these assholes.

"We're gonna have some fun with you baby…you want that, don't you?" I shake my head, looking up into a pair of dark eyes. There is no emotion, no caring nature in those eyes, just pure lust, and I know then that the two men before me are monsters.

I look past the two figures in front of me and realize that they've left the door open behind them. Hope blooms inside me. They take another step forward…they're much too close now, and I know if I want to survive this I need to do something. Fighting the ache in my muscles my body starts to move on its own. I jump up from the mattress trying to run past them, but even drunk the men are faster than I am. I barely make it a couple of feet before one of them grabs me by the arm yanking me backward.

The Luca man pushes me into the second guy's arms. Panic swarms me, my chest heaves up and down and still through it all I know that I need to fight them even if my chances of escaping are slim...I'm not going to go out without fighting.

I might not have the strength I need to overpower them but I have long nails and I use them to my advantage at that moment lashing out with my hand sinking them into his ugly face, well slashing downward. He hisses out in pain, and I relish in that sound.

Of course, he rewards me by backhanding me across the face, pain radiates across my jaw, the impact of the hit making my head snap back. Tears fill my eyes, and before I can recover my arms are roughly twisted behind my back, making me cry out in pain. I can barely see through the treacherous tears spilling out from my eyes, but from what I can see I know I got the bastard good. Five bloody scratches line his face and I almost smile, almost.

"You're going to fucking regret doing that you whore." Another slaps lands on my face, the pain intensifies, and before I can even get my bearings my dress is being ripped down my body in one furious pull, leaving me in nothing but my underwear.

"Fuck look at that little body...I bet she's tight." The Luca man grips me by the chin, his fat fingers digging into skin. I snarl my lip and spit right in his face. He looks at me with murderous rage, and I wonder if this is where I'm going to die.

He wipes a hand down his face and with that same hand he punches me. Literally punches me. My jaw aches at the impact and the copper taste of blood filling my mouth.

"Please...please stop..." I cry, trying to wiggle out of their hold but my futile attempts just seem to ag them on. The one behind me is grinding his erection into my backside and the one in front of me starts smiling while he squeezing my boobs painfully. When one of his hands travel down between my legs roughly grabbing me there another rush of anger floods my system giving me just a little bit more strength.

I grit my teeth and push through the pain. In my final attempt to fight them I throw my head back as hard as I can hitting the guy behind me somewhere in the face. He releases me with a grunt and I use that moment to bring my knee up and kick the guy in front of me between the legs. He falls to the floor, a number of swear words fill the air. Without looking back I bolt towards the door and out into a well-lit hall. I'm out... I'm outside of the cell. I glance back at the man over my shoulder and see out of the corner of my eyes that I can see through the mirror into my cell like it's a window.

They've been watching me this whole time...watching me, seeing me struggle, and cry. Adrenaline floods my body, forcing me forward. I start running, without thought to even where I'm going, only that I need to get away from those men. I hear someone following behind me, heavy footsteps, and words in a language I don't understand.

Once I reach the end of the hallway I take a sharp turn around the corner ready to pick up speed. Instead, I slam into a wall...or what I think is a wall. When I lift my eyes I discover that it isn't really a wall, but a wall of muscled chest.

All the air leaves my lungs at the impact and my knees almost buckle underneath me. Strong arms grip onto me, engulfing me in warmth...in safety. My hands land flatly on his huge chest, and I curl my fingers into his shirt when I hear the two men trying to hurt me approach behind us.

I look up at the face belonging to the body of the man who is holding me. His eyes are gunmetal gray reminding me of the sky before a storm but as he looks into my eyes his gaze softens.

"Help me, please help me," I whisper, my voice trembling. I grip onto his shirt tighter willing him to help me, to save me from these horrible men. He doesn't say a word, he just stares at me, no emotion whatsoever in his eyes. When the heavy footfalls of the two guys chasing me stop behind us, I see his eyes move from mine, and past me to where the two guys are standing.

I feel their presence without looking, and it terrifies me. I pray he isn't going to give me back to them, I don't know what will happen if he does, but I won't just let them have me. No way. I bury my face into the unknown man's chest. His scent washes over me, he smells like expensive whiskey, and cinnamon. Feeling his muscles move underneath my touch...I know he is so much bigger and stronger than those two, he could protect me from them.

An eerie moment of silence falls over us, and my body starts to shake uncontrollably.

"That bitch tried to run boss, we were just going to put her back in the cell." The Luca man interrupts the silence.

"And who opened the cell door for her?" The man holding me ask. His voice is deep and dark, and dread fills my veins at his words. He is not going to help me. He knows I've been here. Maybe he is the one that put me in that room. The one who kidnapped me. Sobs wreck my body at the disappointment. I'm never going to get out of here. I'm never going to be safe again.

"Ivan... boss, we were just going to have a little fun... we weren't going to hurt her..."

"You don't touch the merchandise and by the looks of her fucking face, it seems like you did a whole lot of hurting her," the man named Ivan growls.

One single word stands out from his sentence: Merchandise? I know what the word means but I can't comprehend what it means for *me*. They can't possibly be selling me...or anyone for that matter, right? It's illegal to sell humans, men, women, it doesn't matter.

As I listen in shock to their conversation I realize that I'm still holding on to the man who obviously has something to do with me being here. Why do I feel safe in his arms? I should push him away, fight him like I did the other two men. I should try and escape, but instead, I lean into him for comfort. I feel safe in his arms even though the rational part of my brain tells me I shouldn't.

I enjoy his big hands sprawled out over my back, and the warmth his body gives me and for a moment I can forget the throbbing in my face and the split in my lip. I can forget that I've been kidnapped, and held hostage against my will.

"She tried escaping boss, we had to stop her. Maybe if she didn't try and claw our fucking eyes out she wouldn't look like she does," The other man starts, but Luca cuts him off by clearing his throat as if he knows better than to disobey what the man holding me says.

"It won't happen again boss. We just wanted to have a little fun, clearly, we made a mistake. We'll put her back in her cell, and lock it up."

My body stiffens at his words and my fingers imbed into Ivan's shirt. *Please say no.* I silently say in my head like a prayer. If he gives me to them I'm going to run...I'm going to run as fast and hard as I can.

"I'll take her back myself and if I see you two around her cell again... I'll kill you both. We don't touch the merchandise if you want to fuck something go to the whorehouse," he warns them.

"Of course boss." They both mumble and when I hear their feet pounding against the floor going in the opposite direction of where we're standing I sigh. I cling to the man before me, my fingers refusing to let go of him.

A whimper escapes my lips when he prys my fingers from his shirt and lifts me into the air, holding me like a groom holds his bride... like I weigh nothing at all, and I probably don't considering his size. I briefly catch a glimpse of a large tattoo on the side of his neck before I lower my face so he can't look at it.

He cradles me to his chest like I'm a small child. His skin feels so warm against mine, and I want to sink deep inside him and stay there forever. I twist and burrow my face into his chest. I remember then that I'm completely naked, other than my panties. I've never been naked in front of a man before, and now I've been naked in front of three all in one night.

"Please don't put me back in that room." I murmur into his shirt. He doesn't respond or stops walking in the direction I just came from. He just continues walking as if he didn't hear me at all and with every step he takes I lose a little more hope that I'm ever going get out of here.

Keep reading
GUARD ME

ABOUT THE AUTHORS

J.L. Beck and C. Hallman are an USA Today and international bestselling author duo who write contemporary and dark romance.

For a list of all of our books, updates and freebies visit our website.

www.bleedingheartromance.com

About the Authors

Beck and Hallman
BLEEDING HEART ROMANCE

- CASSANDRAHALLMAN / AUTHORJLBECK
- CASSANDRA_HALLMAN / AUTHORJLBECK
- CASSANDRAHALLMAN / JLBECK

ALSO BY THE AUTHORS

CONTEMPORAY ROMANCE

North Woods University
The Bet
The Dare
The Secret
The Vow
The Promise
The Jock

Bayshore Rivals
When Rivals Fall
When Rivals Lose
When Rivals Love

Breaking the Rules
Kissing & Telling
Babies & Promises
Roommates & Thieves

Also by the Authors

***

DARK ROMANCE

The Blackthorn Elite
Hating You
Breaking You
Hurting You
Regretting You

The Obsession Duet
Cruel Obsession
Deadly Obsession

The Rossi Crime Family
Protect Me
Keep Me
Guard Me
Tame Me
Remember Me

The Moretti Crime Family
Savage Beginnings
Violent Beginnings
Broken Beginnings

The King Crime Family
Indebted
Inevitable

Printed in Great Britain
by Amazon